The Leanin' Dog

By **K. A. Nuzum**

SCHOLASTIC INC.

New York Toronto London Auckland
Sydney Mexico City New Delhi Hong Kong

Thank you kindly to:

Steve van Lier

Holly McGhee

Emily van Beek

Joanna Cotler

Karen Nagel

Alyson Day

Ellen Howard

Dave DiDomenico

Mary Ann Louden

Willard Louden

Ann Keith

Matt Keith

ISBN-13: 978-0-545-20212-1
ISBN-10: 0-545-20212-4

Copyright © 2008 by K. A. Nuzum. All rights reserved. Published by Scholastic Inc., 557 Broadway, New York, NY 10012, by arrangement with HarperCollins Children's Books, a division of HarperCollins Publishers. SCHOLASTIC and associated logos are trademarks and/or registered trademarks of Scholastic Inc.

12 11 10 9 8 7 6 5 4 3 2   9 10 11 12 13 14/0

Printed in the U.S.A.   40

First Scholastic printing, September 2009

Typography by Larissa Lawrynenko

This book was made possible, in part, by a grant from the Society of Children's Book Writers and Illustrators.

To my mom,
Ruth Betty Glenna Cline Weedman Nuzum
1918-2006

Southwestern Mountains of Colorado
1930

1

Just Like I Used To

I SHOVED MY BRAIDS up into my woolen cap, pulled the itchy thing farther down over my ears, and crossed to the cabin window. I touched my nose to the small square of cold glass.

The snow had started up again; it fell thick and heavy like the velvet curtain at the theatre way down in town. I filled my eyes with the sight of it and then scrunched them shut and stretched my arms wide to both sides. Up and down real slow I moved them, like I used to, lying in the deep snow, pushing out perfect angel wings, feeling the cold and the wet seep through the backside of my britches and coat, feeling the snow spill down my neck. I remembered.

My eyes roved over the snow-covered ground. Reading the morning paper was what Daddy called it. I figured four new inches had fallen on top of the old three feet. I saw a coyote had trotted by and stopped to sniff at the base of the big pine that stood at the edge of the front porch. He'd come sometime during the night; his prints looked crusty at their edges. There was a round snuffle print and a fan of snow where he'd paused and stuck his nose down in right ahead of his side-by-side front paws. A magpie had hopped in a circle all the way around the big pine and kept on going out toward the woods. His long tail print followed behind the tracks of his big feet.

Looking out on the calm, white world, a hope started deep inside me. "I can," I whispered to myself. "I can. I can. Just like I used to."

I called up what Daddy said was my stubborn streak and snatched my coat off one of the fat ten-penny nails Daddy had hammered into the wall to hold our outdoor duds and knapsacks. I stuck my arms through the sleeves as quick as I could, buttoned it lickety-split.

My heart started to thud, but I ignored it.

My jaws commenced to ache from clenching my teeth. I ignored them, too.

"I can." I tried to say it in a stubborn manner.

The steel latch on the cabin door was cold as death to my fingers. I'd meet Daddy right outside, I told myself, and say good morning, and he would give me the biggest smile. His eyes would look surprised, amazed, and proud as all get out. I lifted the latch and the cabin door swung out.

Frigid claws of air sliced at my face. My hands flew up to cover my ears under the woolen cap, and I hadn't even told them to.

"I can. I can."

My heart pounded so I thought it would burst through my chest. Out the door I pushed myself and onto the front porch. Nettles of dry snow pelted my cheeks. I looked up and my breath caught in my throat; the sky was so gray, so low. Masses of clouds as big as the continent of Africa rolled past over my head.

Pressing my ears tight against my head, I forced my eyes down to the porch and made myself concentrate on the wooden planks. I tried to step just where the snow had blown off and the boards showed. I pushed my feet past the knothole shaped like a wolf's head. It was smack in the middle of plank number four, counting from the cabin door.

I stepped onto plank number six with the eleven nail scratches in it; snow covered most of them. I made a new scratch on my birthday every year. I had started carving them when I turned four, and the marks from back then were shallow and wiggly. They got deeper and straighter each year.

I forced my feet over my birthday lines and across plank seven and plank eight. There were only two more boards, two more boards to the edge of the porch.

"I can. I can."

But my ears were starting in. The ache commenced, the ache that stretched from my ears to my toes . . . the losing-Mama ache.

"I can." My voice sounded small and raggedy and muffled.

I was almost to the edge. Almost to where the porch stopped and the wide world began.

There was hardly any steam coming from my mouth now. I gasped air in, but I couldn't let it go.

I blinked my eyes, scrunched them tight to stop

their tears; but I told my legs to keep on. And they did, pushing me out to the edge, out to the edge.

The sky seemed to drag on the tops of the pine trees, coming lower and lower, squeezing me and making my head spin.

I lifted my right foot off the porch and hung it out in the air. I commanded my knees to bend; I ordered my right foot to reach for the ground.

I couldn't see the ground for my tears, and my eardrums vibrated with the sobs I tried to hold inside.

"Mama!" The scream blew out of my mouth like the wailing wind.

As I whirled back to the cabin door, I caught sight of Daddy headed for the shed, where he had a deer carcass frozen. He spun around when I screamed, and our eyes met.

He didn't have the biggest smile on his face.

He didn't look proud.

He didn't look surprised or amazed.

2

The Tips of My Ears

I BOLTED INTO THE cabin and slammed the door behind me, slumping against it, gulping air, filled up with shame. Shame just like yesterday morning and the morning before and the morning before that.

I bent myself double trying to make the pain in my chest ease up. I used to go outside all the time when Mama wasn't dead. I worked outside in the garden with her, our pretty garden that was set off so neat and square by the silver chicken wire fence. In the spring we'd plant nice, straight rows of seed, and the breezes would run through my long hair, the bees would hum close to my ears, and it felt fine.

We took long walks in the summer, too, miles from our cabin, way out under the blue sky, so high and wide. I'd lie right out in the open, on the sun-warmed bank of Willow Creek, and Mama and I would pick out pirate ships and elephants in the clouds.

Why, I even went to town like it was nothing, way far down the canyon and up and then out and across the miles and miles of flat land. And that felt fine, too; I used to get excited all over just thinking of the journey.

Now, here I was, I couldn't even get off my own front porch to use the outhouse. At first Daddy had said over and over that when spring came and the air got warm, he was positive sure I'd be able to go about the business of daily life without my ears holding me back and tormenting me. But Daddy hadn't said anything encouraging about my ears for quite sometime now.

How could something dead be such an anguish? The tips of both of them were dead as doornails. Dead like . . . Mama. They had died when she did, frostbitten just like her. Oh, you could still see them, but the only time I could feel them ever since they were killed was when they got cold, and then they ached so and reached down into my heart and made *it* ache so, remembering the dying day, I could hardly bear it. I couldn't bear it.

I scrubbed at the tears on my cheeks with the beautiful, embroidered handkerchief Mama had stitched my initials on for my last birthday, and then I let out a great, shuddering sigh and hauled the chamber pot out from under my cot.

3

Yolks and Whites

BREAKFAST WAS OVER, and I was performing my morning ablutions, as Mama called them. That is to say, I was washing my hands and face. Beyond the cabin window the snow was falling faster and heavier; I could barely make out the first stand of pines and junipers to the west.

Daddy was bundled for his daily trip up the mountainside to check his traps. He wrapped his muffler twice around the lower half of his face and swung the knapsack packed with a water jug and jerky and small, dry apples over his shoulder. He laid his hand on my arm, so light, as though he feared I might break.

"The weather's settling in, Dessa Dean. And the

wind's kicking up. . . . Stay inside."

Our eyes hooked up, and I saw Daddy knew he didn't even need to say that last part anymore.

He stepped out the door, and I gripped the washrag tight and scrubbed at my face until the skin burned.

When I couldn't stand the sting another second, I quit and made myself think on schoolwork needing to be done. I laid hold of the pine dinner table and dragged it with its legs chattering across the floorboards so it set before the woodburning stove. I shoved my chair up close, too, and plunked down.

My tablet lay open upon the table, and I saw that Daddy had written out twenty new spelling words for me to learn. Mama used to be the one to come up with words for me. Every year the snow would start to fly, and then it would pile up, and I wouldn't be able to get to the schoolhouse down in the canyon till spring.

Nobody else could, either. By the first part of December, even the nasty twin boys, the Bradleys, who lived the closest, wouldn't be able to trek through the snow. So, Miss Auburn would close up shop until spring came and all eight of us pupils would make our return. She always said it took her a solid two weeks to get us settled down from the excitement of seeing one another again. Even so, I loved that Mama and I had the great, long winters together to do spelling and arithmetic and read books . . . and to take our long tromps through the thick stands of pine and juniper, through the deep snow, over the windblown drifts, far, far from our cabin.

Winter. That was the first word Daddy had written on the paper. I already knew it. W-i-n-t-e-r. I didn't even have to look as I wrote it. Five times, in cursive. Daddy picked a lot of words I already knew. But I didn't fault him for it. How was he to know? While Mama was teaching me more and more words, Daddy was up the mountain, checking his traps, making sure there was enough food to see us through the w-i-n-t-e-r.

Now he was in charge of both things, keeping food on the table and schooling me. A lot of times his spelling lists had a main idea. I always tried to figure out what it was; I got a feeling for what was on Daddy's mind that way.

Celebration. C-e-l-e-b-r-a-t-i-o-n. Daddy's second word for me.

"T-i-o-n," I said out loud. "T-i-o-n." Mama and I had worked on t-i-o-n words just last autumn. We practiced them while we worked in the garden, digging up the fat vegetables our spring seeds had become.

C-e-l-e-b-r-a-t-i-o-n. I wondered if we would have

Christmas. A lump of sad settled at the bottom of my stomach. Christmas without Mama? I tugged my itchy, woolen cap farther down and pushed my pencil point hard onto the paper.

C-e-l-e-b-r-a-t-i-o-n. Five times in cursive.

Present. P-r-e-s-e-n-t. Too easy. Daddy must be thinking about Christmas, too. If we did have Christmas, I knew what his p-r-e-s-e-n-t from me would be: fudge. We had bought two thick bars of chocolate on our last trip to town with Mama late in the summer past, and she had said I could use the small platter from her best set of china to serve it on. Mama had talked Daddy into spending the extra money on the chocolate, and he never suspected what it was for.

P-r-e-s-e-n-t. Five times in cursive. If we had Christmas, I wondered if there would be a present for me. Mama always saw to that, too. Last year I'd had oranges, sweet like candy and all the way from the state of Florida. There'd been a warm spell right before the holidays and Mama had slopped through the mud all the way to town to get them for me. The year before, it was a big sack of Oklahoma pecans she'd bought before the w-i-n-t-e-r settled in.

I went through all of Daddy's spelling words. His

imagination was threadbare by number twenty. After I'd written r-e-d five times in cursive, my mind was wandering and my eyes were following it to the cabin window and the blowing snow outside. The top of the big pine next to the porch whipped back and forth in the wind; the cabin creaked, and an icy stream of air swept in under the door and chilled my ankles.

I turned the page of my tablet past the spelling words to the recipes, and the yolks and whites Daddy had set for me. "Recipes" was Mama's and my word for addition problems. Yolks and whites meant subtraction.

When I was little and Mama was trying to teach me arithmetic, I hadn't taken to it right off, so she helped me to understand by explaining how adding numbers was the same as following one of her cooking recipes. Just like we took different ingredients and mixed them together to make bread or stew, we could take various numbers and combine them and make something new.

And subtraction, Mama used to say, was just like separating the egg whites from the egg yolks when we were fixing to bake one of her butter cream cakes; you took one part of a number away and got a different, smaller number just like we took the whites away from whole eggs and were left with only the yolks.

Cooking was always one of my most favorite things to do with Mama, and arithmetic came to be another. Why, by the time we got to multiplication and division, I didn't need any fancy names for them; I just took to both like a duck to water. That's what Mama said, and it was true. But I still fancied Mama's old names for adding and subtracting.

Daddy always laid my arithmetic problems out across the page instead of up and down, and no matter how good I was at reading sideways, my mind would only do ciphering top to bottom. I always rewrote them so there were top numbers and bottom numbers. Four hundred eighty-five was what came of setting one hundred eighty-eight on top of two hundred ninety-seven in a recipe.

I was doing a yolks and whites when a baleful gust of wind slammed the front of the cabin and my writing hand skidded across the paper leaving a dark pencil streak through half my arithmetic assignment.

The windowpane rattled and jumped, and suddenly, the wind pulled the door wide open.

I hollered as tiny shards of white ice blasted my face, and the cold air charged in so strong it sucked the living breath out of me.

And all of a sudden, I wasn't ciphering in the cabin anymore. The woodburning stove was gone, and I was crouched in a snowbank, hunched over Mama, trying to protect her from the wind. Trying to talk her onto her feet.

"Please, Mama! Please," I yelled out against the wind. "We'll freeze; we need to walk. Josephine Elvira Hubbard!"

"You go on, scaredy baby." Her mouth was thick and slow and her words all slurred. "I'm staying right here, scaredy girl. I'm staying right here and wait for Jack Frost. You'll see; he's coming, sure."

When I tried to pull her up, she wrenched her arm away and smacked me across the cheek. It hurt twice as much as it would in summer because of the cold. I didn't fault her, though. When Mama's sugar got low, she said things she didn't mean. She did things she didn't mean. We'd made sure to eat a hearty breakfast, and Mama had taken her insulin just as she ought. But now it was long past the time she needed to take more nourishment.

There was no arguing with her when her sugar was low, and so I slumped down beside her, not daring to go look for help for fear she'd wander even farther and be lost all alone. When Mama's eyes closed and she wouldn't talk anymore, I wrapped myself around her to try to keep her warm, and hoped.

Hoped it would be Daddy that found us first.

4

Going Daft

THE SNOW SLAPPED at us from all directions, and the wind howled fierce and mean. Or was it Jack Frost? Coming just as Mama said. My eyes flew open to see.

The wide-open door of the cabin was there before me.

And it wasn't the wind howling; it was me, and my chest ached from it. It was another of my waking dreams, my daymares. I hadn't told Daddy about them. He knew about the nightmares, though, and they were exactly the same. In them I'd be out with Mama, trying to shelter her, hoping for Daddy to rescue us. But he never did.

He didn't come until after.

Until after Mama's body had used up its last reserves of sugar trying to keep warm.

Until after Jack Frost had crept up and taken advantage of her weakened state.

And killed off the tops of my ears.

That's when I'd start hollering and fall off my cot, and Daddy would come and pick me up and talk soft and warm till I could catch my breath and quit crying.

"Look, Dessa Dean," he would say. "I'm putting another log in the stove to warm your ears. You can go on back to sleep now."

The truth is, I was scared to tell Daddy about my daymares. Deep down inside I held a fear that I was daft, and if I spoke out loud about my daymares, it seemed like there'd be no taking the words back, and saying them would make them true, no two ways about it. I had a suspicion Daddy was getting to where daft was what he was thinking about me, too. And that scared me more than anything. If there was two of us thinking it, well, it couldn't help but be so.

I crawled to the door and pulled it closed and jammed the latch up hard to make sure it caught and the door wouldn't blow open again.

My legs wobbled on their way back to my chair. I tugged my itchy woolen hat down, and made myself concentrate on slowing my breathing and figuring what five hundred seventy-four set on top of nine hundred and one came out to. The correct answer was one thousand four hundred seventy-five.

One more arithmetic problem was all that was left to me, and then I could read. Reading was my comfort, for it took me far, far away from the things that frightened me.

Six hundred sixty-two set atop seven hundred sixty-nine. *Two plus nine is eleven, carry the one,* I told myself, and then my heart leaped into my throat; the howling had started up again. Fright jumped through me like a jackrabbit; I thought sure another daymare was come to take me away.

"But it never happens twice in a day, never." And there was my small, raggedy voice out in the air again. "Never." I tried to sound firm.

The howling didn't stop. My eyes raced to the door—it was shut tight—and then to the window. The pine tops were still; the wind had died.

But the mournful sound kept on.

My hands gripped tight on the table edges, but my ears followed the cry. It came from outside. From *right* outside. From out on the porch.

And then there came a scratching on the door.

I jumped out of my chair so fast it fell backward and clattered on the floor.

5

A Lump of Brown

NEVER BEFORE HAD one of my day-mares come ascratching. My knees started to knock again as I crossed to the door. I pressed my ear to its rough wood, listening.

The scratching came. And a soft whine. From down low.

I circled my fingers around the door latch and closed them tight. I didn't feel like I was being taken by a daymare; I didn't feel like I was slipping away. I felt the cold latch in my fingers and the cold air coming in under the door. I heard the scratching and the whining.

I tugged my woolen cap down one-handed and pulled my stubbornness up from deep inside, and I lifted the latch and pushed the door.... It didn't budge.

"Mayhap it was the wind after all; mayhap the wind caused the snow to drift and pile up against the cabin door," I said.

The idea swelled my courage, and I drew back and then butted my shoulder hard against the door. Cold air swiped at my cheeks as the door jumped open a crack, but right away it slammed shut again.

"We'll see about that," I said, and it was through clenched teeth. I backed up to the table and pushed off it to give me a powerful start, and I heaved my whole self square at the door. It swung wide, and I went with it, barreling into the great outdoors.

As my hands flew to my ears, my eyes flew to the big, snow-covered lump of brown that was struggling to its feet smack dab in front of me. I tried to sidestep it, but my feet were going too fast, and the stoop was slick, and so I ran full into the lump and fell square on top of it.

I let out a grunt when I landed, and the lump yelped and squirmed and wriggled out from under me. It took off lickety-split toward the woods.

I pushed myself onto my knees and peered through the curtain of snow.

Why, it was a dog! Not a daymare at all, but a dog had come ascratching at the door. Something was wrong with one of its legs, though. There were four of them, but the right front one acted like it belonged to someone else. It swung wide of the body instead of underneath it, as if it was trying to get away on its own.

"Here, dog," I called. "Come back!"

The dog stopped, and I filled with hope when she turned around. She looked at me, cocking her head.

"Oh, please, won't you come back?" I called to her. "Come back and keep me company?"

The dog stood for a long minute, sizing me up, and I drank in the sight of her.

Fudge-brown was the color of her coat, and the white snow piled up in a broad stripe down her back from her ears to her wagging tail. She was so big, her head was wide and square, and her flopped-over ears were a deeper brown than her body. She had them pricked, listening to me, and they looked like they were straining to stand up all the way. Her tail was long and feathered along its bottom edge. She was beautiful.

As I watched, the dog tilted her muzzle high, and across the distance I heard what she'd said.

"Roo!"

And then she loped away from me, into the woods, that right front leg trying to go north while the rest of her headed west.

"No! Wait, oh please, wait."

I scrambled to my feet, and I ran, without thinking, to the edge of the porch. I jumped off; I was going after her! I was going after her, and then, then my burning ears seized me so strong I tumbled to my knees. My eyes held fast to the woods, though, searching for the dog.

But there were only snowflakes. Silent snowflakes.

I limped back inside the cabin and sat down before the stove and pulled my trouser leg up over my right knee. It was skinned and bloodied from hitting the sharp-crusted snow. I felt the same way on the inside.

From the small bookstand next to Daddy's cot I fetched my history book and tried to settle into how Roman Emperor Constantine had been responsible for spreading the Christian faith all about the ancient world, but the questions racing through my mind and the longing that gripped me kept me on my feet, gimping back and forth across the cabin and pushing wide the door time after time.

"Do-og. Come! Come, dog," I shouted out through the snowy air again and again. But my voice sounded even smaller than before.

Injured!

ELEVEN WAS THE number of times I opened the cabin door and called for the dog. Twelve was the number of steps it took me to get from the table to the door. Twelve steps to, twelve steps back equals twenty-four steps each trip. Therefore, the correct answer to how many steps I took looking for the dog is: eleven times twenty-four steps or two hundred sixty-four.

If I had taken those steps in a straight line, I told myself, *I would have gotten to the edge of the woods, and had I called the dog from there, she might have heard and come back.* The thought brought tears to my eyes.

Oh, I wanted that big, fudge-colored dog to come back.

I rocked to and fro in my chair.

Where had she come from? Why had she come to our porch?

That was when I stopped crying and sniffed and sat real still thinking. I slapped my forehead and said right out loud, "Dessa Dean, you are a dumb bunny."

I marched to the door, gave it a shove, and then plunked myself down on hands and knees on the porch.

The first thing my eyes lit on, right smack in line with the door, was the lay the dog had made. I reckoned it to be about three and one-half feet around; she had tromped the snow down and curled herself up real tight against the cold. My own footprints dashed right through the middle of it from when I chased after her. I hadn't taken any note of her bed then, but now I could see her big ol' footprints around the edge of it and see how the snow in the center of the lay was smooth and melted down from her warm self lying in it. New ice crystals were already forming at its edges.

But resting wasn't the first thing she had done, I

saw. Her prints came up the porch steps, and traveled first to the side where the big pine stood. There was a little puff of snow before her front paw prints and five inches of bare green on the lowest pine bow overhanging the porch; she'd been asniffing.

From there the dog had padded over to the other side of the stoop and sat down. A smooth, fan-shaped patch of snow behind her sit print showed she'd been wagging her tail.

I traced four different trips she'd made from one side of the porch to the other. Seems she'd been pacing just like I had.

As I stared at her tracks, something else jumped out at me all of a moment: the print from her right front paw didn't go so deep in the snow as the others; she hadn't put as much weight on that foot, and yet the claw prints showed more clearly, like you'd expect to see from a deeper, heavier step. The right front foot was landing flatter and more splayed out than her left front, and didn't set in line with the others. She was most certainly favoring that paw. That was the leg that swung out on its own when she was arunning.

She was injured, sure, and mayhap stopped at our

cabin, looking for help and comfort; and here I'd scared her off.

I scoured the entire porch on hands and knees, peeking into each and every print; there was no sign of blood.

"Well, that's a comfort," I said.

I stood up, wincing, for my scraped knee had stiffened.

"Do-og." I sent my voice out into the fading light, floating it out above her paw prints all the way to the woods, hoping. "I'll help you if you come back. I can help you if you'll just come on back."

I stayed still for a long moment, listening but hearing nothing, and then went back inside.

The deep, cold shadows came so very early in the winter; it was too dark now to try reading or any other close work.

Daddy was firm that I would have to wait another year before I could light the fancy, red glass kerosene lamp or any of the lanterns on my own, so when the afternoon's light began to fade it meant my studies were done for the day, and it was time to start supper before it got too dark to see.

I nudged the pine table back to where it belonged and checked the venison steak Daddy had cut and brought in that morning. It was thawed but for its center.

I stuck a thick log into the stove's belly to get it real hot for cooking. This winter for the first time Daddy said I was old enough to stoke it by myself; I often wondered if I was old enough only because Mama was dead.

Keeping my ears trained to the door to pick up any whining or scratching, I hauled the big stewing pot out from the lower cupboard and set to cutting up potatoes and carrots we had stored from last summer's garden.

Each time I finished a potato, I peeked out the door in case any barks or yips had been muffled by chopping and slicing noises.

The porch stayed empty.

Eventually, I got the pot filled with sufficient meat and vegetables for two nights' worth of supper. I added water for broth and three pinches of salt, two of pepper, then clanked the lid on tight and set it to cook on the stovetop.

It wasn't very long before the cabin was filled with

the rich, meaty aroma of the stew. That's when I got
my idea.

With a fork, I speared chunks of meat in the pot,
fishing for the most tender, and plopped half a dozen
of them into a small pan with some of the broth. Then
I bundled myself up good and pulled my cap down and
carried the pan outside.

"Do-og." I stretched my arms out as straight as they
would go, way past the edge of the porch, and waved
the pan around so the breeze would catch the stew's
savory smell and carry it out to the dog's nose in the
woods.

"Come to supper, dog."

Stamp! Stamp, Stamp!

B UT SHE DIDN'T.

I stayed out as long as my ears could bear the cold and then nestled the steaming pan of meat and broth down into a patch of snow and trudged back inside. How was it the cabin seemed a little bigger and a little emptier each time I came in from hunting the dog?

I hung my coat back on its tenpenny nail and then stirred the stew with my long-handled spoon so it would cook evenly and not stick or burn, just as Mama had taught me.

I believe it was a full minute before I realized I wasn't only hearing the spoon scrape against the sides and bottom of the pot.

I was hearing the pan scrape across the porch!

My heart gave a leap.

"Dessa Dean, you're a wily girl." I congratulated myself as I hurried my coat back on and scooted to the door.

"Hold up now," I said. "You scared her off once."

I reined myself in and tiptoed up close to press my ear to the door. Yes sir, she was licking and lapping at that pan like crazy; I heard it clink and clatter from one side of the porch to the other.

Lightly, I slid my fingers around the latch and slowly, slowly, oh so, I lifted it and eased the door open. Never before had I noticed what a mighty creak that door had.

Outside, the clinking and clanking stopped.

I edged the door open a teensy more, pale light from the stove fire jittered onto the porch.

A shadow jumped back into the dark.

I stretched my neck out like a mud turtle and peered behind the door.

"Here, dog. It's only me. You remember me."

I spoke ever so slow and gentle.

A scuffle answered me. A small scuffle.

And then a stamp. Stamp, stamp, stamp.

It was not the sound big ol' dog paws would make.

It was the sound of little feet, little hind feet.

I was familiar with that sound.

I jerked my head back quick and slammed the door.

But too late.

8

A Warning

THERE WAS A spattering against the door, and a second later the skunk's harsh perfume wafted in from below. Instantly, my eyes teared up, and I commenced to choke. There I stood, dumbstruck, crying and wheezing until finally I thought to wet down a dishtowel and plug the space between door and floor. But already the delicious smell of stew was gone from the air, crowded out by skunk.

Boots tromped onto the porch. I heard the pan rattle and roll across the planks.

"What the devil?"

Daddy's voice sounded right outside, and my heart

jumped as the door pulled wide and his dark outline appeared.

"Dessa Dean? What in the Sam Hill is going on? What's the good cooking pan doing outside?"

Daddy stepped into the cabin, the pan swinging from his right hand.

"It stinks to high Heaven out there."

He took a sniff and coughed.

"And in here. Don't dare tell me you been feeding varmints again, girl."

Daddy closed the door and nudged the wet dish-towel back in place with his boot toe. He turned to me. His face and voice were dark.

I didn't often get a fright from him, but at that moment he looked so awful big, and I felt all shrunk down. When Mama was alive she was middle-sized, so at times like this she would step up in front of me and say, "Now, John, calm yourself," and I felt sheltered from Daddy's large proportions. But Mama was gone, and somebody so small as me wouldn't dare tell Daddy to calm himself.

"No, sir," is what squeaked out of my mouth.

"Then why was the pan out on the porch, and why

am I choking on the stink of skunk?"

"Oh, Daddy!"

And in an instant, all my excitement about the dog flooded back, and all my fright ran off.

"A dog came round today. A beautiful, big, fudge-colored dog. And she came right up on the porch. She has a hurt front leg, Daddy."

"No dogs in these parts, Dessa Dean."

"Oh, but there was! Cross my—"

My words stopped in the air when my eyes met with Daddy's, for what I saw there was: daft. I stared at the floor for a minute, shamed, and then deep inside I felt my stubborn streak start to stir. I raised my chin.

"I can prove it."

Worry replaced the harsh judgment in Daddy's eyes.

"Let's just get on with chores, Dessa Dean," he said in a soft voice. "Supper ready?"

He walked over to the stew pot on top of the stove.

"Please, Daddy. Please, won't you light the lantern and come take a look? Her prints are all over the porch."

He looked at me with his head cocked just as the dog

had done. He rolled his lips under and gave a little nod.

"All right. Let's see."

"Well, I'll be."

Daddy was squatted down next to her paw prints, holding the lantern high.

"Got big feet. They don't fit the dog's weight; it's light. Feet that big should have close to a hundred pounds on top of them. This dog weighs in closer to seventy, I'd guess."

Seventy pounds! Why, that was still big, and it was twenty pounds more than what Daddy reckoned I weighed. I'd really skinnied down since Mama died. The way Daddy said it was that I'd lost pounds since my ears started tormenting me.

"You're right about that front leg ailing her," Daddy said. "Acts like a ruined tendon, the way the toes splay out and the foot sets down flat. That's why she doesn't weigh what she should; she's having trouble hunting with that injury."

Daddy rocked back on his heels.

"You're still a fine tracker, Dessa Dean. Why don't you come up the mountain with me tomorrow? Plenty of tracks to keep you busy all day."

I dropped my eyes and shook my head.

"No. I best not."

The sigh that came out of Daddy pained me.

"It's not . . . not what you think," I said. "It's due to the dog." I so wanted there to be a different reason, a new reason, not to go up the mountain, not to step off the porch.

"The dog?"

"Yes, sir. I'm hoping she might come again tomorrow, and I could make friends with her."

Daddy straightened up and stepped to the door.

"Let's have a look at what you got accomplished in your schoolwork today." Daddy turned to me and locked his eyes onto mine. "And, Dessa Dean, if that dog comes back, you're not to mess with her. She's wild, and that means unpredictable. She could have the hydrophobia or something equal to it. You hear, girl?"

"But, Daddy, I—"

"And don't dare set food out again or we'll have more than skunks to deal with; the bears are out hunting for food in between storms. Setting edibles out on the porch is begging them to come calling. Hear?"

Scootching

THE WIND HOWLED and battered against me, and Mama just lay there in the snow, so silent, while tiny snowflakes collected on her dark eyelashes. I wrapped my arms tighter around her and turned my head to look back the way we'd come. The wind seared my cheeks, and my eyes filled up with the sight of snow blowing across our snowshoe tracks, erasing our path home.

The grief that was upon me was so heavy when I woke from the nightmare, I was limp as a rag doll. I felt Daddy's arms around me; I felt the warmth from the stove, but the only thing I could do was lie droopy and weep.

When finally all my tears were gone and my eyes were sore and dry and only the last shudders were left inside me, Daddy tucked me under the quilts, and I fell asleep to the sight of the gray dawn light creeping into the cabin and the sounds of Daddy preparing to set out for the day.

I was hot, hot when I woke in the morning. Daddy had stoked up the stove for the sake of my ears, and I was buried beneath three quilts, even my head, and when I poked out from under them, I saw the sun had filled up the cabin, adding its own heat, for the storm had moved on.

I threw the covers back and rolled my itchy woolen cap partway up my head, and when I did, I heard a scratching noise, and I knew right off it was the dog come again. She was back!

I tugged my cap back down and ran toward the door. I grabbed the latch, and then, I remembered. Remembered Daddy's words: "Dessa Dean, if that dog comes back, you're not to mess with her. You hear, girl?"

I let go the door latch. I forced my feet over to the pantry shelves and brought down the loaf of bread. I unwrapped the blue-bordered white towel that was keeping it fresh and cut a thick slice. I spooned golden honey from the glass jar onto the bread, spread it clean from one edge to the other, and folded the slice in half.

Came a scratching at the door.

I dragged my chair up real close-like to the table to hold me in, and set down.

A whine sadder than the night wind arose on the far side of the door, tickling at my determination.

I gave my chair a powerful shove backward and ran for the door.

As slow as I could bear, I pushed it open and stuck my head out.

"Dog?"

There she stood, just behind the door.

Our eyes met, her legs braced, ready to run.

"Oh, no," I said softly, and shook my head just barely. "Please, stay."

I looked away so she would know I didn't plan on attacking her, or falling on top of her again.

"I'm so happy you came back. So happy."

I eased the door open a little more—that dad-blamed creak!

"Wouldn't you like to come in, dog? I'll cook up some breakfast for you."

She sat down and thumped her tail.

A smile dropped onto my own face.

I waved for her to come, and I stood aside so she'd have room to pass.

The dog tilted her head back and kept her brown eyes trained on me.

"Rrrooo," she sang out in her deep ol' voice. It wasn't a bark, particularly, and it wasn't a howl, exactly.

I'd like to, but I can't quite, was what I thought she meant by it.

With my eyes cast to the porch planks and my hand outstretched, I took two baby steps nearer to her.

She stood up again.

"Rroo," she said, her whiskery muzzle tilted up, and she turned toward the steps.

"Oh, no, please, please stay. I won't hurry you, I promise. Cross my heart." I x-ed my finger over it and took one giant step backward.

The heavy muscles in her shoulders relaxed, and she sat back down, facing me.

I crossed my ankles and lowered myself slowly,

slowly, oh so, to the porch so I sat Indian-fashion. I leaned back against the wall and cocked my head so I could sneak sideways peeks at the dog without making her feel like I was staring at her.

"My name is Dessa Dean," I said. "I wonder what yours is. I wonder if you've ever had a name."

Her tail thumped.

I thought maybe she was getting used to me a little. I wanted her to know my voice and trust it, so I kept talking.

"What made you come, dog? It's due to trapping that I'm here. My daddy worked in town when I was real young, but all the jobs dried up, and he wasn't able to keep food on the table like we needed, and so my daddy moved Mama and me away up here where there's plenty of game. We have food for the table and pelts to sell, is what Daddy says."

The dog eased herself down in a patch of warm sunlight. She stretched her front legs before her and settled her chin on her paws. She let out a deep sigh with a little whine hidden inside it. Her eyes closed slow and lazy-like.

I stayed put for another minute, and then I

scootched forward, a bare two or three inches. The dog opened one eye and blinked at me and then closed it.

I scootched again.

This time she opened both eyes and lifted her head.

I looked down at her on the porch.

"It's okay, dog. I won't hurt you. I want to be friends."

She stretched her nose out toward me, and it went crazy, sniffing quick and loud.

Slowly, slowly, I moved my hand closer to her.

Oh! That big brown nose was cold as ice and nice and wet. And her saggy jowls that brushed against my hand as she sniffed it all over, they were velvety soft.

Her tail thumped, and she laid her head back on her front paws, and when I took my next scootch, she didn't move a whit.

Half In, Half Out

THE FIRST TIME I ran my hand over the length of her, she ducked her head and flattened out her floppy ears, like she expected I was going to strike her. But the next time, she didn't flinch at all, just rolled her eyes back to follow my hand as it moved, and finally, on my hand's third trip, she laid her head on her paws and just smiled.

She'd been living the outdoor life for quite some time, I reckoned. I had petted a house-kept dog down in town at one of Mama's and my friend's, and its fur was sleek and silky and required fancy food and a bed before the fire to keep it that way.

This girl was smooth, but her fur was stiff, kind of

wiry, like it was accustomed to standing up to harsh conditions.

She had variety to her, too. Her ears were dark, chocolate-brown, her head a shade lighter, and at the back of her neck there was a ruff, a reddish ruff that interrupted the smooth flow of her fudge-colored coat, like water going over rocks in a creek.

"Ruff?" I asked.

The dog didn't even twitch.

"That's not the right name, is it, girl."

I lay down on my side, facing her.

She licked my nose.

Her tongue looked huge right up close like that.

"Licker?"

She lay her head down again.

"Reckon not."

Just under her throat, at the top of her chest, there was a small whirl of white, like a tiny snow-storm.

"Stormy? Snowflake? Blizzard?"

The dog let out a deep sigh.

"Those aren't right, either, are they."

I smoothed my hand over the top of her big left

front paw. Her nails were black and a touch raggedy from digging.

Oh! I'd completely forgotten about her hurt foot, about her tendon, her strange-acting leg.

Her eyes followed me as I moved to her other side, but she stayed put.

I picked up the right paw.

Real lazy, she wiped her wide pink tongue across the back of my hand.

With a light touch, I pressed her paw all over, in spot after spot.

The dog yawned.

I ran my hand a little harder over the underside of her leg, pressing in at the shoulder, working my way down.

When I got to just above her wrist joint, to where Daddy suspected the hurt tendon was, the dog let go a tiny yelp and pushed up on her feet right quick. She limped to the edge of the porch and looked back at me, sorry-like, as if to say she'd trusted in me and I'd let her down.

"Oh, dog!" I pushed the words out beyond my rising fear. She couldn't leave again, not like this, not with the feeling she wasn't safe with me. Why, she might never come back with that as the last thing on her mind.

"I was only wondering," I said. "I wanted to help." I patted the plank next to me. "Come here, girl. I'm sorry. We'll just keep it your business. I have something private myself, something I won't talk about with anybody. Come on, now. Please, dog."

She cocked her head and looked me in the eye, as if to say, *You promise?* She didn't leave, but she didn't come onto the porch any further, either.

"It's not poking you need, is it, dog. It's warm food and a place to feel safe."

Slowly, slowly, not looking straight at her, I stood and edged my way to the cabin door.

"Now," I said in my gentlest tone, "I am going in and heat up some stew for you, with lots of meat and gravy, and I am going to leave the door open so we can still talk. If you were inclined to, dog, you could come in from the cold. This could be *your* safe place, too."

That girl stayed at the porch edge. I kept her in view as long as I was able, and as soon as I was all the way inside the cabin, I ran on tiptoe to the window and peeked out at her. She caught the movement, and for just a moment I thought she was going to bolt off after all. The muscles in her haunches tensed, and she made a slight turn away from me. But nice and easy I waved to her and started up my talking once more in a real conversational tone. The dog sat down, and I got out the good cooking pan that I wasn't supposed to be feeding varmints from, and I pushed that thought way to the back of my head. I scooped out a humongous portion of meat and gravy from the big pot, and I stoked up the stove as quick and quiet as I could and set that stew to simmer.

As the food heated up, its aroma floated across the cabin. The dog stood and stretched and padded right over to the threshold of the door. I smiled at her.

"Smells fine, doesn't it, dog?"

She wagged her tail at me and her mouth opened and her tongue rolled out and she drooled onto the floor.

"Famished, is what you are." I stirred the stew to spread out the heat nice and even and stuck my finger down into the middle to make certain it wasn't too hot. I carried it four modest-sized steps closer to the door and set it down.

"Come on, girl. Come and get it."

The dog wagged her tail again.

"Come on. Come here. It's good, I promise."

She didn't budge, but lifted her muzzle and looked past her long nose at me.

"Rrrooo," she told me.

"All right," I answered, and slid the pan three more steps closer to the door. "How's that?"

Her nose stretched out toward the stew, and her whole body quivered, she wanted food so bad.

"Oh, dog, I only want you to trust me just a mite more. You can do that, can't you, girl?"

She wagged, and I nudged the pan so it was just two of my steps inside the cabin. "Will that do?"

And then, why, she did the strangest thing. Something that wasn't at all like what you'd think a dog would do. That girl lay down with her belly almost flat to the floorboards, and she commenced crawling toward the pan. She scraped over the planks as though she was trying to be invisible. Even when her front half arrived at the stew, her back half still lingered on the porch. It made no never mind to her, though; she set to lapping up the gravy and then gulping down the chunks of meat like there was no tomorrow.

I heated her up a second serving, and then a third, and I put two more logs in the stove and then two more after that, for the cabin was cooling down considerable, what with the door still opened wide to accommodate the dog's back half that wouldn't come in off the porch.

I think her front end would have kept right on eating so long as I kept on serving, but an uncomfortable, prickly sort of question sprang to my mind concerning the amount of stew that remained for Daddy's and my supper. When I looked into the big pot and saw the carrots and taters in a little heap on the bottom, not even floating—for I had ladled up most all the gravy for the dog—well, I slammed the lid on the pot and quick prayed a prayer: "Oh, Lordy, please don't let Daddy notice the lack of meat and gravy. Amen."

I looked over to the dog, and my spirits lifted. She was sound asleep. The pan was tipped on its side, and that girl's nose was right inside of it. She must have quit licking and commenced dreaming at the same exact moment.

I couldn't help but smile, and I pushed worries about Daddy's dinner out of my mind. Schooling was

the thing I had to be concerned with, for if there was
one thing that made Daddy's stern look come on, it
was me neglecting my studies.

"Your education was mighty important to your
mama, Dessa Dean, and the fitting way to honor her
memory is to take your learning serious." That's what
Daddy said on days when he thought I had been pokey
and not industrious enough.

I tugged on my heavy coat, for I was shivering outright from the chill air filling up the cabin, and from
the pockets I fished the gloves Mama had knitted for
me winter last. Of a sudden, I felt surprised for even
with the cabin door wide, there was only the quietest
ache in the tips of my ears.

Just as quiet as I could, so as not to disturb the dog,
I inched the table across the floor and up close to the
stove. That girl was so tuckered out, she didn't even
twitch. I set the chair so my backside would get
warmed by the fire, and I stuffed two more fat logs into
the stove's belly. Then, opening my tablet to a fresh
sheet of paper, I set to my second spelling lesson for the
week, which was to make all the words from the list fit
into sentences. I was full up with things to say, and my

thoughts tumbled out so quick, my fingers wore out trying to get everything down.

> *1. The <u>winter</u> brought a heavy load of snow onto our porch, but it also brought the big fudge-colored dog up there.*
> *2. The dog showing up on our porch was just like a <u>present</u> for me and made me want to put on a <u>celebration</u>.*

I felt mighty proud working two of the spelling words into one sentence like that, and as I looked over the rest of the words, why, it seemed like every one of them was just made for a sentence about the dog. Even r-e-d didn't seem so old and tired anymore. For that one, I wrote: *The dog is fudge-colored mostly, but around her neck, like a mane, is a <u>red</u> ruff, but Ruff is not her name. I checked.*

I went back and scratched out the *I checked* part, still in wonder about how all those words seemed made for dog sentences, and then I thought how Daddy's spelling lists sometimes had a theme to them. Could it be he knew the dog was coming and had worked out the spelling words to suit? With all the discouragement he'd offered up about her the night before, it didn't seem likely. But mayhap someone else, someone like God, or Mama, up in Heaven, mayhap one of them knew and figured on softening Daddy's heart toward the dog by giving him words for the spelling list. Well, mayhap.

So, there I sat, feeling cheery and comforted, and the next moment, why, I almost keeled over with fright. Out of the blue, the dog let go the meanest, loudest bark and sprang up, making her food pan clank and roll across the floor. That dog bolted out the door and onto the porch, barking and growling, making me tremble.

I dashed after her, tugging down my woolen cap, my mind seizing on the idea that she smelled a bear acoming, or even a mountain lion. Thoughts raced through my brain: Could I haul the dog inside and pull the door shut and latch it before either one of us got eaten?

I peeked out, and there, at the edge of the porch, stood the dog, legs braced wide, her right front paw setting flatter than the others, her hackles standing straight up in a ridge down her spine. Her pale lips were drawn far back to show off her sharp, angry-looking teeth. Fierce and long, a growl rumbled up from way deep inside her, and another sharp bark came on its heels. She was ready to fight.

My own eyes followed her wide-eyed stare out through the dimming afternoon light, out across the field of snow, out to the pine and juniper, and what I saw set my heart to racing more than any bear or cougar ever could.

11

Shotgun

I T WAS DADDY. Coming out from the woods. He was trudging through the snow, eyes cast down, looking done in, and it didn't take but that first glance for me to see that his sled was mostly bare; only one or two skins were piled on it and the rest of the space was taken up with traps to be fixed or oiled. Daddy's luck with the traps must have been sorry; that always made his step slow and the rest of him all slumpy.

When the dog barked the second time, Daddy's head lifted and he stopped and stared right at the dog.

"Oh, Lordy," I groaned, and then I yelled so the dog could hear me over her own voice. "Shush now, oh, shush, now. You have to stop, girl. Stop."

But she didn't.

When I looked out to the woods again, my breath caught; Daddy was running toward the cabin and hefting up his shotgun.

"Daddy! Oh, no, no. Daddy, no, *please*." I hollered to him at the top of my lungs, and my shrieks made the dog go berserk. She lunged from one side of the porch to the other, snapping her jaws, barking like a killer. Her eyes were locked on Daddy.

The whole world slowed down and down to a crawl. I felt the blood pound hot in my temples; I watched Daddy point the barrel of his gun skyward. He fired it, and I saw the gun recoil into his shoulder.

The quiet winter air cracked into a million splinters with the shot.

Startled, a black-as-pitch crow gave a harsh cry and flapped into the sky.

The dog flinched and bounded off the porch, stumbling when her ailing paw hit the hard-packed snow, her right leg trying to run off on its own. I watched her dash toward the canyon, running away from Daddy.

Running away from me.

Before I could yell out, or grab on to the door, a daymare swooped down and carried me off. Carried me off to watch Mama die again.

How long it was before my mind let me come back to feel Daddy's warm, strong arms rocking me before the crackling fire in the stove, I don't know.

But in only a breath's time, more sorrow poured into my heart and flooded the whole of me. I'd just lost Mama for the hundredth time, the thousandth time, and now, back in the wide-awake world, the dog was lost to me, too. For good and for all. She wouldn't come back, not after Daddy scaring her off with his gun.

"Dessa Dean. Dessa Dean," Daddy whispered my name over and over, and he sounded scared.

Why? And then I recalled: He had seen me slip away into a daymare for the first time. My arms and legs went stiff with shame. I turned my head away from him and kept my eyes closed. I didn't want to see how daft he thought I was.

"Dessa Dean. Thank God, child. Did that dog hurt you? Dessa Dean?"

I shook my head hard.

"You certain? The way she was lunging and growling, and then I saw you fall to the porch. She didn't bite you? It's important; she could have the hydrophobia, and if you got bit . . ."

"We're friends; she wouldn't hurt me." My voice was all shaky. "She was just protecting me, and guarding our home."

Daddy let out a *hmph* noise.

"Well, if you wasn't hurt, what caused you to fall?"

His arms loosened around me, and he set me up straight on his knees. I saw he had my writing tablet clutched in one hand; it was opened to my dog sentences page.

"Dessa Dean? What *was* that? What happened to you out there?"

I sat quiet, feeling dread push sorrow out of its way.

Daddy gave me the littlest shake.

"Tell me, girl." His voice was skinny with worry.

"A daymare." A shuddering sigh came out of me. "They're the same as the bad night dreams I have about Mama, but they come in the day. They come when I'm awake."

I couldn't hold the tears back; they burned down my cheeks and dropped onto Daddy's big, chapped hands.

"Good Lord, child." He pulled me in close to his chest, rustling the pages of my tablet, and he held on to me tight. "Why didn't you tell me before?"

"I was scared to."

"Scared? What was you scared of?

I was silent till Daddy gave me another bitty shake.

"Scared you'd think I was daft." I whispered the words. "I didn't want you to think I was."

Daddy sat very still.

After a time, I began to wonder if he had heard me.

I could feel his heart beat, my head lifted and fell with his breath.

At long last, Daddy set me up straight once again. His eyes had a stern look to them.

"You are not daft, Dessa Dean. Do you hear me, girl?"

I nodded.

"You are not daft."

The way he said it made it sound like an order, or like a schoolwork assignment.

"All right, Daddy," I said. I didn't know if a body could just decide not to be daft, but, oh, I wanted to try for Daddy. I reached down deep inside myself and called up my stubborn streak. *I won't be daft.* I thought it loud and strong in my head. *I'm not daft. I'm not.*

I was shouting at myself so loud inside my head, I didn't think I'd heard right when Daddy spoke again.

"I was wrong to run that dog off," he said. "That dog can stay, Dessa Dean."

I sat up even straighter, like a fence post, and threw my arms around Daddy's neck and squeezed him hard.

"Oh, Daddy, thank you. Thank you so. She's the best dog. Truly, she was just trying to protect me and protect the cabin. And she doesn't have the hydrophobia at all."

And then I remembered.

The dog was gone.

I slumped against Daddy, and the tears jumped from my eyes again.

"She won't come back." The words sobbed out of me. "She'll be too scared."

"Well, now, I reckon she'd come if you warmed up some of last night's stew and set it out and called to her, Dessa Dean."

"That won't work." I said it with my head hung low.

"That dog's skinny. She'll come back when she smells your fine stew."

"I fed her most all the stew already, Daddy. There's only vegetables left."

I felt Daddy's arms tighten up and heard his voice do the same. "You fed that dog my supper? After I been out all day in the freezing cold, fighting to put food on our table? You did that, girl?"

"Yes, sir. I did that."

Daddy was real quiet for a long minute, and then he let out a heavy sigh.

"I'll go out to the shed and cut some venison steaks for supper tonight then, and I'll cut a slice for the dad-gum dog. You go on and stoke up the stove and get the frying pan hot."

He didn't sound tickled about it, but he was acting in an encouraging manner.

"Yes, sir." I walked over to the woodpile next to the stove, and my heart dropped all the way to the floor. "Lordy," I whispered to myself. There was only one skinny log left. I had gone through two days of wood to keep me and the dog's front end warm.

"Could you get more wood, too, Daddy?" I asked

in a small voice, my back turned to him.

"More wood? Dessa Dean, I just brought a load in this morning."

He stepped over next to me and stared at the bare floor. "I stacked two days' worth of logs right there. You couldn't have burnt up that much wood in a single day. Dessa Dean?"

The edge to his voice was sharp.

I took a deep breath. I kept my eyes on the floor, but I spoke up strong and honest.

"The dog wouldn't come but halfway into the cabin; she was just too skittish to bring her whole self in. So, what I had to do was leave the door open, and after she ate, why, she fell fast asleep, half in and half out, and the cabin got mighty cold, and I was worried my ears might set in, so I had to keep burning the wood. I had to."

Daddy slumped down on his chair next to the table. He ran his hand over his forehead. He looked plain weary.

"Dessa Dean," he said. "That dog has cost me, in food and fuel and worry, and she was here less than a day. Could be it's not such a wise thing to encourage her after all. She don't remember how to live with humans, could be she never knew. She might never tame down sufficient to stay inside with us. I got a hard enough time providing for our needs without chopping wood for a wild dog."

"I'll do it! I'll chop extra wood, Daddy." Soon as I heard the words out in the air, I shrunk up inside and quick dropped my gaze back to the floor. But not before my eyes had met Daddy's, and I saw in his the very same thought I was having: *I can't even get myself off the porch, how could I chop any wood?*

Daddy took my hand and pulled me alongside him. After a long moment, he lifted my burning face up and looked me in the eye.

"Could be having that dog around will ease the ache in your ears, Dessa Dean. That's worth extra chopping."

12

Scaredy Baby

DADDY WAS FIRM that I set down and eat my own supper before trying to lure the dog back. My stomach was jumping so with the hope of her return, it felt like the bites of deer steak and the forkfuls of leftover vegetables bounced up and down inside me every time I swallowed. I kept at it, though; Daddy was a real stickler for leaving a clean plate because of the considerable effort it took for him to fill it. "Waste not, want not" was one of his favorite sayings. He said it most on nights when we had squash. Squash was never a favorite of mine or Mama's. But Daddy said it was a mighty dependable vegetable; neither bugs nor lack of sun nor lack of water discouraged it from growing, so Mama and I planted a variety every year.

At long last, our supper plates were empty, and I jumped to washing the dishes and finished them up but quick. I was ready.

"Daddy, you reckon I should fry the steak up for the dog? Or would she like it best raw?"

He shook his head. "She's not going to care. She's a dog, Dessa Dean. Leave it raw."

I pulled on my boots and bundled myself in my heavy coat, whooshed my hands into my gloves, and dropped a nice, thick slice of venison into the dog's bowl.

I yanked my cap far down over my ears and my forehead; my eyes barely stuck out.

Onto the porch I stepped and made certain the door was shut tight behind me. I didn't want Daddy having to do any extra wood chopping before morning.

I took a deep breath of the bitter, cold air and called out. "Dog, oh do-og." Like a wish, my voice floated into the night.

I waved the pan up and down and back and forth and around and around, so the breeze would carry the aroma as well as my heart's desire to the dog.

But that dog didn't come.

I stepped to the very edge of the porch; the toes of my boots dangled in thin air.

"Come on back," I said. "Daddy won't shoot off his gun anymore; he promised he wouldn't, and he's a man of his word, dog. Do-og."

I closed my eyes and let my ears search the black night for the barest sound. There was nothing to be heard except the icy air stirring the tops of the pines.

I trudged back inside the cabin and rubbed my ears; they were aching.

"Daddy? I believe she's taken a liking to cooked meat. I'll just fry the steak a tad, and mayhap that will bring her back."

Daddy looked up from repairing his traps. "Don't dally, Dessa Dean. It's time you was in bed. If the dog don't come round tonight, she will tomorrow. She might need some time to calm down."

"Yes, sir," I said, and set to heating up the skillet quick as I could.

A few minutes later, I plopped the cooked steak back into the bowl and carried it out to the porch again. This time, I went directly to the edge, and clutching the bowl in both hands, I waved it out into the air, far as I could reach.

"Dog! Come and get it. It's delicious, and it's for you. That stew must have worn off a long time ago; you got to be hungry by now, dog. Come on. Dog."

I stayed perky and gladsome for as long as I could, but in my thoughts, I began to reckon that dog had run a long ways off when the gun fired, and she was too far distant to smell the venison or to know I was calling to her. If I wanted that dog to hear me, to know she could come on back and get something to eat in safety, I would have to get off the porch. Get off the porch and step into the dark night, make my way deep into the bitter cold, through the long stretch of nothingness, out to the canyon rim where the dog had disappeared.

I pinched my eyes closed and stretched my head forward into the blackness and leaned my shoulders out, too. A pulse began to beat in my temples, and my breath wouldn't come but in short gasps.

"Dessa Dean, you get in here now." Daddy's voice boomed through the wood door.

I whirled around, and I *ran* to that door. I yanked it

wide, and I threw myself into the warm, safe, small cabin.

Relief filled me up bottom to top.

And then shame crept into my heart and my head, for I knew even if Daddy hadn't hollered, I wouldn't have gone after the dog. I knew if ever I was going to see her again, it would depend on her mustering up the courage to come back. I was a scaredy baby.

Onto my cot I crept, and deep, deep under the pile of quilts I scrunched, so none of me stuck out in the light. Inside my head, I called to the dog over and over to come on back. I told her I couldn't come fetch her, I just couldn't, and I begged her to come home and be my friend.

Even with the boredom of counting backward from one hundred, I couldn't fall asleep. I rolled and twisted and turned and flopped. When Daddy had blown out the kerosene lamp and stretched out on his own cot, and when he snored his first snore, then I wriggled out from under my quilts. Only glowing embers were left in the stove's belly; the wooden planks of the floor were cold, cold on my bare feet as I crept across the cabin to the door. It took fourteen-and-one-half tiptoe steps for me to get there.

I closed my fingers around the cold steel of the latch and lifted it up and caught my breath with the clink it made; it was terrible loud in the quiet. But when Daddy let out a big blow, I knew it hadn't disturbed him. Daddy had a range of noises he could make when he was sleeping, and I was familiar with them all.

One night, just out of the blue, when Mama was still alive, he came up with a brand-new one, a puff with a word in it: two. Well, sir, I couldn't help but giggle the first time I heard it, and there in the dark, Mama answered with a giggle of her own. She crept out of bed and lighted a candle, and took my hand and led me up close to Daddy's face, and we watched him for quite a little while. That's how I came to know how he made each of his noises. The puffs came when he breathed out through his mouth but kept his lips closed; they'd kind of billow out and then lay back down. The big snorts came from breathing in through his mouth and his nose at the same time, and generally, those woke him up and made him roll over. Sometimes, they made him cough.

I slipped onto the porch and pushed the door to behind me. There was only a tiny patch of wood free of ice, and I had to stand one foot on top of the other. The chill wind cut through my nightshirt like Daddy's skinning knife would.

"Dog!" I whispered. "Do-og, come here, girl."

Something rustled beneath one of the junipers close to the porch, and my heart jumped with hope. I stared my eyes into the blackness, but my ears were already telling me it was someone a good deal smaller than the dog I was hunting for.

A humpbacked raccoon waddled out, hardly sparing me a glance before he got along with his business on beyond the cabin.

"Dog," I called one more time, but there was no answer.

My feet were so cold they would hardly tiptoe back inside, and my fingers were stiff, so when I let the door latch down, it made a loud clunk.

Daddy rolled over.

"Get into bed," he grunted.

Well, I did, and after a time beneath the quilts, I was toasty warm again, but I still wasn't asleep. I could tell Daddy was back to a peaceful slumber, so once more, I crept across the cabin, lifted the latch, and crowded my feet into the little circle of bare wood on the porch.

"Do-og. Do—"

Before I even finished the whisper, Daddy's voice put its foot down.

"Dessa Dean!"

I'd been back under the quilts again, wishing hard that I would fall to sleep so my heart would have a rest from hoping and aching, when, out of the blue, a porch board creaked. It sounded like my birthday scratches plank, groaning under the weight of something heavy—heavier than a coon. I swear my ears picked up the sound of the dog sitting down and swishing her tail back and forth over the iced snow.

I skittered out of bed quick, like a spider caught in somebody's shadow, and this time, why, it only took me *nine* tiptoes to get to the door, due to my speed.

I cracked it open and peeked out.

Nothing.

"Dog. Dog," I whispered.

But too loud.

"Dessa Dean, you get up one more time, I'll tan your hide."

I didn't get up again.

13

12 x 8

WHEN THE MORNING finally came, Daddy was in a bad humor. I could tell by the way he snapped his covers back to the foot of his cot. I kept my eyes half closed in the pale gray light, pretending to be asleep still. He let out a vexed sigh and set up on the side of his cot and rubbed his eyes. Daddy sounded worn out before the day had even started, and I was sorry for keeping him up the night before.

Still, I felt a rush of cheer when he pulled his britches up over his long johns, pushed his feet into his boots, and swung open the cabin door, for mayhap he'd spy the dog out there, or at least some fresh paw prints.

I held my breath, but his feet didn't pause, they clomped off the porch and away from the cabin.

Even when Daddy came on back and stoked up the stove and set thick-sliced bacon to sizzling in the skillet, I pretended to be fast asleep. When he rattled the spoon in the honey jar, I pictured him slathering all that golden sweetness over a thick piece of bread, but I kept on lying still. When my belly rumbled, asking to get on up and get filled, well, I stayed beneath the quilts, breathing deep and slow to be convincing.

It wasn't only that I didn't want to face Daddy's stern look. Truth be told, I didn't feel a spark for starting the day. Not with the dog still gone. Even under the quilts, the cabin felt bigger and emptier than it had with just her front half in it. That girl had filled it up and my heart, too, and now both places felt hollowed out.

After a spell of chewing sounds, I heard Daddy slide his breakfast dishes into the washbasin, heard the flannel of his shirtsleeves slide smooth into the arms of his deerskin coat as he bundled up. I heard the metal traps clank against each other when he lifted them from the floor. Last thing before Daddy left, he walked over to my cot. For a long minute, his shadow lay across my face, and then his boots tramped off, the cabin door creaked, an icy blast scraped my cheek, and he was gone up the mountainside.

It was that rumbling belly of mine that finally talked me out of bed. That, and knowing I had school-work to do. That, and knowing if I was still lying abed at the end of the day, there might be more to face from Daddy than his stern look. But mostly, it was a teeny lick of hope concerning the dog's return that brought me to my feet.

I peeked out the window to the porch, but she wasn't there, so I decided to attend to my hunger pangs straight away. On the counter next to the washbasin, three crispy slices of bacon were laid out on a plate along with a double-thick hunk of bread. The bread was smeared edge to edge with the biggest gob of honey, just how I liked it. What Daddy meant to say by the gesture was that he wasn't nettled with me any longer; a smile came into my heart.

A little greater hope for the day came with it, too. I pulled the top two quilts off my cot and floated one down into a nice big square of sunlight on the cabin floor. The other, I wrapped around myself. While I ate my breakfast and took a sunbath, I set out a plan in my writing tablet for the remainder of the day.

1) Get dressed.

2) Bundle up.

3) Go out on the porch and holler for the dog.

4) Do spelling work.

5) Bundle up.

6) Go out on the porch and holler for the dog.

7) Do ciphering.

8) Bundle up.

9) Go out on the porch and holler for the dog.

The first time I stepped outside, my eyes right away lit on a midden of pinecone scales at the edge of the porch. There was quite a little pile, right in the middle of a patch of sunshine. Somebody had enjoyed breakfast and warmed himself in the sun, just like me. A step closer made me certain it had been a red squirrel. It was his little back paw prints that let me know it. Five toes, gathered up three in the middle and one off by itself on each side, and no print from a heel pad. There he'd set in the early morning sunshine and stripped five piñon pinecones of their scales to get at the teeny, tasty, tan nuts that nestled on the scales' top sides.

But of the dog, there wasn't a sign. I looked at the lay she'd tramped down the day before, iced over and forsaken. My spirits drooped. Her paw prints were old, too, and showed only what she'd done yesterday. She'd not been back.

Still, I hollered for her; it was part of my plan. The only answer that came, though, was from a black-capped chickadee.

"Ho-hum," it called.

And that was how I felt.

I went back inside and daydreamed my way start to finish through my spelling lesson. I underlined the action word in each one of my dog sentences and printed "V" for "verb" above the word. But while my writing fingers did that, the rest of me was remembering the feel of the dog's fine fur and the scratching sound her claws made on the cabin door when first she'd introduced herself.

After I had all the verbs squared away, I went back and circled the main character in each dog sentence

and printed "S" for "subject" above it. But the whole
time my hand was circling and printing "S" here and
there, my mind was off thinking of how sweet waking
up mornings would be if I was to reach my hand out
from under the warm quilts and get a soft, friendly lick
from the dog first thing.

The second time I went out on the porch, the air
was colder and snow had commenced falling. I tugged
my itchy, woolen cap down all the further.

"Dog! Do-og."

Not even a chickadee answered me. All the critters
were hunkering down, out of the way of the storm.
Still, I scanned my eyes out toward the canyon and
back toward the wood, straining to pick out a feathered tail, or a red ruff through the white veil of falling
snow. There was nothing.

By the time I trudged back inside to do my ciphering, I was shivering from the cold, and my hope was
shrinking.

Daddy's assignment perked me up, though, for it
called on me to come up with story problems that
would show I knew my twelve times multiplication
table. Twelves are the hardest, I swear. I think how

hard the twelves are is due partly to how worn out a body is by the time a body makes it from the ones all the way through the elevens. But I set to the twelves with enthusiasm, for it was another opportunity to talk about the dog.

If it takes <u>twelve</u> steps for a girl about my size to cross over to the door from the woodstove, in order to look for the dog, and a girl about my size goes just the <u>one</u> time, how many steps are involved altogether? The answer is twelve, and this story problem just goes to show that 12 x 1 = 12.

I started out making all the story problems about taking steps to look for the dog, but that became wearisome and plain drab somewhere around 12 x 4. So, I branched out.

If that dog came to stay with me for a duration of twelve days and made me so happy I smiled from one corner of my mouth to the other every day she was here, and if that girl came to stay for twelve days, eight completely different times, how many days would I have the biggest smile on my face? The answer is ninety-six, and this story problem just goes to show that 12 x 8 = 96.

By the time I was up to 12 x 12, I was so worked up about the dog, I couldn't sit still another minute. So, just a mite ahead of schedule, I bundled up and trotted out onto the porch.

The sky was a dark, dark gray. The wind was howling something fierce and blowing the new snow sideways, so I couldn't make out even the first stand of junipers. The old, frozen snow was blowing up, too, and bits of ice stung my cheeks and made my eyes water.

My excitement withered. The dog would never hear me call over the wailing wind. She wouldn't see me, even if she was looking, through all the sideways snow. Sending a message to her nose was about my only chance, I reckoned, and that would only work if she was still in the vicinity of the canyon, in the direction the dad-gummed wind was ablowing.

Inside I trudged and banged the door tight shut. First off, I stoked up the stove, not just for heating up the meat, but for heating me up also.

Before I stepped out the door again with last night's portion of steak, I glanced up at the sky. The clouds were rolling in through the trees, moving toward the cabin like huge, shapeless ghosts. Suddenly, I felt too small, and my eyes got dizzy from not being able to see anything steady, only the moving clouds, the rushing clouds, the ghosty clouds coming on.

But the dog. *Oh, the dog.* Down deep inside myself I reached, searching for my stubborn streak. It took quite a minute to locate, for all my uneasy parts were heaped on top of it. But it was there, waiting, and I pulled it up with all my might. My stubborn streak pushed my shaky legs out onto the porch; the light had dimmed so I couldn't even make out when I crossed the wolf's head plank or my birthday scratches plank.

Out, out to the edge I shuffled, with the bowl stretched far in front of me, and I thrust it into the snowy air, past the last board, out to the west and then to the south. I waved it particular hard toward the canyon in the east.

I strained my ears. A howl? A bark or whine? Paws padding across crusted snow?

Nothing.

There was only me and the wind and the ghosty clouds.

14

Forty-nine Days

"WAKE UP! DESSA DEAN? Wake up, girl."

I opened my eyes, and it was black as pitch, and there was Daddy's voice, full of worry, shaking me awake.

I was confused for quite a little minute about where I was and confounded as to what time of day it was until I remembered that I'd come back inside the cabin, after hollering for the dog without success, and laid down on my cot under all the quilts to warm myself. But now, Daddy must be home from trapping, and it must be suppertime. *Uh-oh*, I thought.

I set up and stretched my arms.

"Are you ailing?"

I could hear that Daddy's voice was really asking was I going daft even though he'd told me not to.

I shook my head, though he couldn't see it in the dark.

"No, sir. I got cold calling for the dog, so I burrowed under the quilts, and I guess I fell to sleep."

"Well, then." His voice was considerable relieved.

"She didn't come back," I said. "The dog didn't come back." I could hear my tone sounded accusing, though I didn't intend it.

"I don't reckon a dog with a lick of sense would come out in a storm," he said. "She's probably hunkered down, waiting it out. Likely tomorrow she'll show up."

But I could hear the doubt hiding behind those cheery words.

He patted my knee under the quilts.

"Dessa Dean, do you know it's almost Christmas?"

Something in my throat caused me to swallow real quick. I peered up through the darkness toward his face.

"Yes, sir. But, without Mama—will there be

Christmas this year?"

The question weighed a million pounds; it squished my voice into a tiny squeak, and it seemed to smoosh Daddy's entirely. I felt him sag, and the dark set heavy on us both.

After a long sigh, his voice came back.

"There'll still be Christmas." He sounded just like when he told me not to be daft. "You always love this time of year, Dessa Dean," he said. "Your mama did, too. She wouldn't want us to give up on it."

He gave me a two-armed hug.

"Let's haul out the decorations and spruce the place up."

Something inside me started to ache, thinking of Christmas, remembering Christmas with Mama. I wanted to stop it before it got too bad, or too big.

"What about supper?" I asked. "I should get to cooking."

But Daddy wouldn't be set back on his heels.

"Supper can wait," he said, and he stoked up the stove, lit the big kerosene lamp, and from next to his bookcase he hauled out the wooden trunk that held our Christmas treasures.

"What about my twelves?" I offered. "I only got to eleven times twelve today, Daddy. You better have a look."

But Daddy didn't pay me no never mind. He just blew the thick layer of dust off the lid and lifted it up.

I couldn't help but edge closer to see. Right on top, rolled like a scroll, was the Advent calendar Mama had made years and years ago when I was only five. Keeping track of the days leading up to Christmas was one of my most favorite parts to celebrating the season.

The background of the calendar was made of red felt and was most of a yard long, that is to say, three feet. Daddy lifted the calendar from the trunk and unrolled it. The fancy braided cord of green, for hanging it up, was stitched to the corners of its top edge, and the top one-third of the red felt had the backsides of twenty-four shiny, silver snaps sewn all over it. On the bottom two-thirds of the red felt Advent calendar, Mama had sewn twenty-four little pockets of red gingham, scraps left over from a tablecloth she'd made. Each pocket had a hand-embroidered date, starting from December the first and going clean through December the twenty-fourth. And, each and every pocket held a symbol of the Christmas season sewn from pieces of material from Mama's scrap box, stuffed to plumpness with cotton batting and provided with a snap on its backside.

I knew with certainty, for I had counted untold times during every Christmas season, that there were three purple satin wise men; three camels of tan corduroy; one denim chest to hold the frankincense and myrrh that the wise men brought along for the Baby Jesus; three woolly white sheep made up of cotton from the general supply store down in town; one deerskin shepherd with a brown pipe-cleaner staff; three angels of pure white, 100 percent cotton that Mama had sewn our pillowcases from; three gold linen trumpets; one star of Bethlehem crocheted of sparkly silver thread; a deerskin donkey and ox; a brown felt manger; one Baby Jesus of beige brocade; one sky-blue wool Mary; and one green flannel Joseph. Each morning after breakfast, as soon as December started, Mama would let me slip that day's treasure from its pocket and snap it onto the red felt. On December the twenty-fourth, that is, Christmas Eve, I wouldn't snap anything up. Then, late at night, when Mama was pretty certain it was past midnight, we'd sneak out of bed and snap the Baby Jesus up on his real, true birthday. Mama was so clever, she had planned it out and sewn it so that when all the figures were snapped on, they made an entire scene. A manger scene. Mary and Joseph stood over the manger, the Baby Jesus lay snapped inside it, the donkey and ox were snapped on behind Joseph, standing with their heads bowed, the three wise men were gathered close by, and on like that. It was perfect.

"I'm afraid I don't know the exact date, Dessa Dean," Daddy said. "Your mama was always the one kept track." Behind his words this time, there was a touch of consternation.

Without the teeniest pause, and without thinking it over, I just up and said: "Today is December the twentieth."

Daddy's mouth turned up in a bright smile.

"Well, now, Dessa Dean, how'd you come to be so certain?"

Oh, how I wished I could call my words back. I tried to jump over them and over Daddy's question by changing the subject of the conversation.

"I was thinking I'd make some cornbread muffins

to go with supper tonight."

But he wouldn't let it lie. I wasn't the only one with a stubborn streak.

"Dessa Dean? How do you come to know the right date?"

There wasn't anything for me to do but say. I took a deep breath and let it out in a rush.

"Mama froze forty-seven days ago today. On November the third. So, today is December the twentieth."

With those words, it was as if all the frigid air of winter swept into the cabin and froze *us* solid.

A booming silence hovered around us, and it was so loud, I thought my eardrums would burst. Short, hurried breaths were all I could drag into my lungs; I could feel a daymare stomping toward me. I flung one stiff arm out toward Daddy, and I felt him catch hold of me and pull me onto his lap. He held on tight while the pain my words had sparked burned its way into my bones.

A long time later, after the flame of the kerosene lamp had flickered and gone out, when only orange embers glowed from the stove, Daddy lifted me up and carried me to my cot. He laid me down upon it and pulled the quilts up under my chin. He didn't scold me for not making cornmeal muffins; he didn't scold me for not making any supper whatsoever, nor for leaving off on my twelves table. With his rough fingers, real gentle-like, he just smudged the tears from my cheek and crossed on over to his own cot. Its legs squeaked as he set down on it, his boots thunked onto the floor one after the other, a long sigh drifted up from his heart into the dark, and then I was asleep.

15

Angel

"DESSA DEAN! Wake up, girl, wake up!"
There was Daddy's voice shaking me awake. My heart skipped, for it seemed as though things were repeating themselves. Was I stuck in one of my daymares? That was the question that jumped into my sleep-addled brain. What if Daddy just kept waking me up and telling me it was almost Christmas, and what if I was forever stuck counting up Mama's dead days on the Advent calendar? I squeezed my eyes tight, trying to keep everything invisible.

"Dessa Dean, wake up right this minute!"

Daddy sounded very large. I pushed my eyelids up, expecting to see only darkness. But there was the outline of Daddy's face, and he was smiling. Grinning, more like. A great relief washed over me, for I realized it must be morning if I could make out his choppers, and that meant it wasn't yesterday's evening at all, but a brand-new day.

"Get up this instant, and come have a look." Daddy tossed the quilts off me, my shoulders scrunched up, bracing against the cold.

He strode toward the cabin door, and I shuffled my bare feet along behind him. And then, why, he threw the door wide open. Frigid air slapped my cheeks and bare legs. I tugged my itchy, woolen cap down below my earlobes. My kneecaps began to knock against each other.

"Look there, girl."

Daddy pointed his finger at the porch, down at the snow on the porch.

My eyes were still bleary with sleep; I was just peeking out through slits, really, and besides, the dawn's light was still dim. I didn't see a thing worth looking at.

"What?" was all I could think to say.

"Open your eyes and see. Your dad-gum dog has come back."

Well, I surely don't need to say that hearing that
news woke my entire self up but quick. Lickety-split, I
went down on all fours, and, sure enough, there were
new dog paw prints from one side of the porch to the
other. She'd had been apacing again, to and fro, to and
fro. And, there were new melted spots in her lay, too.
She was back! That girl was back.

The atmosphere in the cabin was downright gladsome. It felt almost like one of the special mornings
when Mama and Daddy and I would bustle about trying to get everything done so we could set out for a
shopping spree in town.

Daddy tackled the morning chores with a
vengeance; carving the day's meat, frying up some
breakfast bacon. And without my saying a thing, he
brought in four armloads of wood instead of the regular two. I stood out on the porch the full time, hopping
from one cold foot to the other and hollering for the
dog.

She didn't come.

"She won't come," I said, when I couldn't take the
cold a second longer and scurried back into the cabin. I
backed up to the stove.

"I doubt she will, so long as I'm here. She'll be recalling the scare I put into her." Daddy flipped the bacon over in the skillet. "I reckon after I set out, she'll come round. Be a good idea to have some breakfast ready for her. I brought in a strip of venison; you can gravy it up with the bacon grease here. Be a fancy meal even for a big city dog."

Naturally, as soon as Daddy disappeared into the pine and junipers, I bundled up and scooted on out to the porch and set to hollering some more. Even though the dog didn't come right off, I didn't feel discouraged, not even a whit, for I knew it was just a matter of a little bit of time before I laid eyes on her again.

I thought it best to get right to my lessons so I would have plenty of leisure to spend with the dog when she did show. I skittered the pine table across the floor so it set before the stove, and I plopped myself down on a chair and flipped through my writing tablet to a fresh page.

Tried and tried again to concentrate is what I did, but my brain wouldn't cooperate, not a lick; it was out on the porch waiting to see that dog come bounding through the snow. My ears were distracted, too; they strained so hard to pick up the teensiest noise outside; why, I felt sure if they could, they'd jump off the sides of my head and roll over to the door. Even my eyes strayed from the clean sheet of paper, and finally, I let go a sigh and allowed them their own distraction.

They wandered right over to the Christmas trunk that still set open on the floor. And, of a sudden, while I stared at it, why, I got the itch to decorate up the cabin after all. It would be a way to show the dog how happy I was that she was back. It would be a kind of a c-e-l-e-b-r-a-t-i-o-n.

I knelt down beside the Advent calendar and ran my fingers over its bright gingham pockets. I was in such a cheerful frame of mind that the calendar seemed back to being the happy treasure Mama had intended that it be. *Why*, I thought, *today is December twenty-first; it's the first day of the dog's return.* I slipped a cotton sheep from the twenty-first pocket and snapped it up near the top edge of the red felt. It made me smile to see it there, and quick like a bunny, I snapped up all the treasures from the days before it, from the twentieth clear back to the first. When I was all done, the donkey, the ox, two sheep and their shepherd, two angels with trumpets, one wise man, and the Baby Jesus's manger were all in their rightful places.

I plucked my coat from its tenpenny nail next to the door and draped it over the back of my chair and then slid the braided hanging cord of the calendar onto the empty nail. I stood back and admired Mama's handi-work, as I had time and time again.

Back to the trunk I went then, for there were still more decorations I wanted to set out. The next Christmas treasure my eyes lit on was a parcel about the size of Mama's loaf pan, wrapped up tight in green velvet. Mama had paid a pretty penny for that velvet at the supply store down in town. The reason she'd invested the money was because of how precious the thing wrapped up in the cloth was.

I reached out to the velvet bundle, and while an ache started up inside me, a want, twice its size, sprang up, too. I stroked the deep, soft velvet, and my eyes wouldn't leave off watching the material turn from dark to light as I slid my fingers first against the grain and then with it.

I scooped up the bundle and set it on the floor before me. Careful and slow, I undid the neat bows of twine—

one at the top, one in the middle, and one on the bottom—that Mama had tied after Christmas last year.

The very air felt solemn and regardful to me; it was akin to being in a church. I set both my hands lightly to the velvet and began to unroll it. The fabric unwound across the wood floor like a narrow swath of meadow grass growing toward the stove. After four complete turns, the velvet was out straight. At the very end of the cloth was the treasure it kept safe: a beautiful angel. An angel fashioned from a thick log of piñon pine. Daddy had carved it for Mama one Christmas before I was even born. Leastways, that's what Mama told me, and I had always taken it as truth. Daddy, she said, had spent an untold amount of time searching for just the right piece of wood, one with no borer tunnels, one with no knotholes. When he found it, he set to shaping it into a perfect angel.

Every year for as long as I could remember, I'd start pestering Mama to get the angel out as soon as the snow started to fly. And, after Christmas, I would beg Mama not to pack her away again just yet.

Her skin was a smooth swirl of light tan and medium tan, the different shades twisted and melted into and out of each other in the natural way of wood. Her tiny feet stood on tiptoe on a round base. Angel robes draped her grace-filled form, looking fleecy and comfortable, just what you'd like to wear in Heaven.

I ran my fingertips over her open wings. They curved up toward the sky as if she was lighting to Earth, as though they had just given a last, gentle flutter to help her touch down. And the feathers themselves, oh my. So many, many, many feathers carved in each wing. Every year I tried to count them, and I always came up with a different number. One year she had forty-seven on the right wing and thirty-nine on the left. Then the very next year, it would be forty-eight on the left and fifty-two on the right. Whatever the true number, each feather fit snugly alongside and above and below another. They formed such a perfect piece, I always thought that if only a single one went missing, likely, in real life, she wouldn't be able to fly. Her bare angel arms were spread wide like her wings; they reached out in a welcoming manner, as though they expected to wrap around somebody in only a minute or so.

The fine braids of her hair were even tinier and more delicate than the feathers of her wings; how had

Daddy managed that? There were three like braids on each side of her head, and they were all caught up together in a tall, smooth roll at the base of her neck. I traced their crisscrosses with my fingertips.

Suddenly, I saw something that had been lost on me before that moment: This was how Mama sometimes wore *her* hair, for special occasions—like Christmas. It was Mama's hair Daddy had modeled the angel's after. And then a question, like a lightning bolt, flashed in my mind, and my eyes darted to the angel's face . . . to . . . Mama's face. For that's what it was; how had I not seen it ever before? *Due to my having Mama's natural features to gaze upon every day, that's how,* I told myself. But now I saw that the angel's high cheekbones were like Mama's; her fine lips showed a little bow at the top like Mama's had when she was smiling just a little smile. And her eyes. The angel's eyes had the soft almond shape of the eyes of a deer, just like Mama's.

Tears jumped from my own eyes and ran pell-mell down my cheeks, and a heavy blanket of sad sagged down over my whole self.

But, all of a moment, before my misery could grip me any harder . . . came a scratching at the door.

16

Return

I HELD STILL, FOR my ears buzzed, straining so to capture the sound. And there, it came again. A smile spread across my face, and it was such a huge smile, my cheeks began to ache right off. Well, sir, real careful I set the angel atop the bookcase, and then my feet jumped into action. I slid right across the floor, at least twelve steps worth of sliding. It came to my mind that I ought really to slow down so as not to fright the dog, but there was no stopping any of my parts.

Therefore, instead of being cautious and smart about greeting her, why, I threw the door wide and jumped myself right onto the porch, without even a thought to snugging down my woolen cap for the sake of my ears.

My eyes were sprung wide to catch sight of her, and the winter air hit them hard; my eyeballs felt like they'd turned to cold glass. But they could still see. They could still see that dog.

Oh! What a sight, it was like eating one of Mama's buttercream cakes. That is to say, my eyes gobbled her up. They took in her big brown eyes, and caught how they widened so the whites showed when I sprang right in front of her. Her feathered tail gave a wag and then dropped in alarm. Her four giant paws, the front right moving last, scrambled to gain purchase on the icy porch, and her legs bent so she could turn and run away from me again.

"Oh, no, no. Don't go, please, don't go." I whispered the words and, at the same moment, I eased down to my knees, hoping to look small and less frightful, and I opened my arms wide, just like the angel.

Well, that girl stood stock-still, and then she tipped her muzzle up, her eyes looking into mine.

"Rrooo," she said, and quick as summer lightning, she bolted into my arms.

The size and the weight of her knocked me flat before you could say "What in the Sam Hill," and in the split second after I landed on my back, the dog set to giving my face a thorough scrubbing with her soft, warm tongue. I kept turning the other cheek, but she wouldn't let up.

At long last, at very long last, I gave her a gentle, but powerful shove backward so I could set up and see something more than her long velvet nose.

Once I was right side up, I laid my hand atop her brown head and looked her in the eye. "Welcome back!" I told her. Time and time again, I ran my hand over her silky head and through her wavy ruff and down the length of her broad back. It's what I did instead of licking.

After a long while of stroking her and each of us getting comfortable with the other, I stood up nice and slow, talking in a calm manner all the while, and took a couple steps toward the door. "Come on in, girl," I said. "It's nice and warm in there."

Her tail began to wag once again, and she followed me right inside.

I left the cabin door open for the comfort of her

back half, and I stoked up the stove for the comfort of all *my* parts. Into the skillet with the thickened bacon grease, I slid the venison strip and commenced heating up one scrumptious doggie meal.

I could sure-fire tell that girl was hungry; as I stood before the stove, sliding the skillet back and forth over the hot burner so as to melt down the grease, she paced to and fro behind me, whining out tiny whines. When the cooking aroma got real strong, she set down on her haunches and gave the back of my knee a nudge with her long nose. Her big brown eyes smiled up at mine, her tongue rolled out, a little bit of drool plopped to the floor, and, in a polite voice, she encouraged me to hurry up.

"Boof," was exactly what she said.

Well, I couldn't help but return her smile, and I swear, I felt so cheer filled, I could have popped.

I swirled and smeared the slice of meat through the grease and cut it into bite-sized chunks before dishing it up in her bowl and setting it down before her.

There was a quick minute of chomping and slurping, then, bang, the pan was so clean I could have put it away in the cupboard.

That girl looked up at me and thumped her tail on the floor.

There was no mistaking, she was still feeling empty.

The only meat left was what Daddy had sliced for our dinner. But the very last thing in the world I wanted to do was set Daddy and the dog off on the wrong foot all over again. Serving up Daddy's supper to the dog, well, that would be the very thing.

"Maybe that's enough, girl. You don't want to overdo, your first day back."

She cocked her head, listening real careful.

She whined.

I chewed on my lower lip for a minute, hoping for an idea.

I got one. Over to the pantry shelves I skipped and retrieved two garden spuds from the storage bin.

There was still plenty of bacon grease, so I fourthed and then eighthed the potatoes into the skillet and mixed them around. Slathered in gray drippings, even I couldn't tell they weren't chunks of meat.

If the dog knew, she was too polite to say. In a matter of seconds she had licked the pan clean once again.

"This time I'm serious," I told her. "You could get

a sour stomach eating any more. Especially when it's something you don't usually eat."

She seemed to be in agreement, for she allowed her tongue one more spin around the inside of the pan and then walked over before the stove.

For a long moment she stood still, like she was thinking what to do next, and then, that girl commenced walking in a small, tight circle. Round and round she went, nose to tail. I laughed right out loud, I got so tickled watching her go. At that sound, she stopped and looked at me like *I* was the one doing something mysterious and silly-looking.

But after a moment's pause, back to it she went, and, as I kept watching, light dawned, and I realized that dog was doing exactly what she would do, or a coyote or a wolf would do when one of them was set on taking a nap in the great out-of-doors. She was making a bed, tramping down the long grass of the prairies and the woods, flattening it out real good so it would be comfy to lie on.

But the wood floor wasn't cooperating. The dog stopped her circling and started ascratching at the planks with her front claws. And then, of all things, she commenced growling at the floor as she dug at it. I reckoned she was plain aggravated not getting the result she was accustomed to.

Finally, though, she seemed resigned to the stubborn nature of the wood floor, and she flopped down upon it, laid her chin on her front paws, and let out the biggest sigh I'd ever heard a body give. Wasn't but the blink of an eye, and that girl was asnoring.

The temperature inside the cabin seemed to be dropping mighty close to the outside temperature, and I wondered if, now that the dog was snoozing, I might dare to close the door.

So, on tiptoes, I crossed the room, nine and one-half steps, and eased the door toward closing—but, that dad-blamed creak!

The dog jumped right onto her four feet, and with her right front paw hitting flat and limpy, she charged toward the door.

I edged backward, keeping myself between her and the door, and spread my arms wide across it, like a barricade, and I shot out the first words I could think of. "Look there," said I, and pointed to the Advent calendar. "See that sheep? That sheep is the twenty-first of December sheep. I put it up this morning to mark your coming back. Everything's fine."

"Boof!" hollered the dog, and she barreled in behind me, her long nose bumping me aside, and set to scratching at the bottom of the door like crazy.

"Say, dog, how about another tater?" I wasn't giving up.

But the dog would have none of it; she was in a true panic. She paced the three or four steps from the door's front edge to the back, tripping over her own feet, whining the while in a pitiful manner. Over and over again, to and fro, all the time sniffing and nudging at the door and digging at its bottom edge.

I was all set to just keep the door shut and wait for the dog to wear down, for I couldn't bear that she run off again. But at that moment she looked up at me, and I understood the dog needed to get out as sorely as I needed to stay in; her brown nose was scraped down to pink, and the tiniest red seep of blood showed on its tip where she had pushed and slid it against the door trying to open it.

I didn't want to, and my hands trembled as I reached for the latch, but I lifted it up and steeled my heart to watch the dog disappear.

17

The Christmas Stars

BUT SHE DIDN'T. Soon as I'd got the door open wide, she set down before me and, looking me straight in the eye, she gave me a loud, one-word ear chewing.

"Boof!"

That was it. Back before the stove she trotted, circled twice, and flopped down.

I just stood right there, pretty near struck dumb with surprise. Then, I raised up on my tiptoes, in a kind of a shrugging manner, lowered back down, and set to stoking up the stove against the cold.

Even though the dog hadn't seemed at all taken with the Advent calendar, I thought, with the door left open, and after a refreshing nap, mayhap she'd take more notice. So, after warming myself before the fire, over to the trunk I went to set out the rest of the Christmas treasures.

What remained were the beautiful stars Mama had crafted from the tops and bottoms of tin cans full of such as beans and peaches. Two or three times each year, when we made the trip to town, Mama would go all out and buy some canned goods. Daddy always grumbled over their high cost. "You're going to land us in the poorhouse, Josie," he'd say. But Mama would smile her prettiest smile and say, "Why, John, just think of a bowl of sweet peaches! Besides, Christmas isn't so far off; we'll need new stars to hang." That's when Daddy would shake his head and wander off to look at shiny steel traps. But, truth be told, we all of us were glad for the change in diet. It was exciting to eat something we hadn't grown, or that Daddy hadn't trapped or shot. Come the first night back from town, Mama would bake up some of her delicious, crumbly corn bread, open a large can of red beans, season them just so, and we'd have ourselves a feast. And for dessert, there would come the promised peaches, dished up in Mama's fancy china bowls.

When the cans were empty, Mama would snip their tops and bottoms free. The cans she used in the garden, to shade tender sprouts, or to hold up wobbly ones, but the round ends, she turned into shining stars. With her tin snips she would cut long, skinny strips from the lid's edge in toward the center, and then she would twist and curl those strips so you would never ever guess the thing had started out flat and plain on a can of beans. Each year she would take one of the lids and work it so it could hold a button in its center, like a gem in a ring. Mama always let me sort through her button jar and pick one I thought would look the best in the middle of a star, and she'd work and curl and furl the strips of tin into a snug, beautiful nest that held the button and showed it off like it was a diamond.

Christmas season last, I had chosen a green button from a dress of Mama's that she had abandoned to the rag pile. The button was as big around as an Indian head nickel, but not flat. Rather, it was round like a berry, and covered over with slick and shiny green satin. Mama had thought it was a good choice; she gave me a little smile and a nod when I held it out for her to see.

A body had to be delicate in picking up the stars, for as beautiful as they were, they were that much sharp, and it was easy to prick or nick your finger on the metal edges if you squeezed too tight. Each star had a circle of thread tied at its top, thread that matched the color of its button, if it had one, so the star could be hung before a window to catch the sunlight and make shimmery, dancing patterns on the walls and floor for hours a day.

I lifted the green-button star from the trunk and tiptoed it thirteen steps past the dog over to the kitchen cupboards. Up on the cutting shelf I set the star, so I wouldn't get sliced, and bending my knees, I sprang up and used my arms to hitch me further, so I could sit right up beside the star. I picked it up by the thread and stretched up to the threepenny nail sticking out from the top of the window frame and looped the thread on over. Honest, I always got the most special sort of feeling when I hung the stars each year. It was akin to having the say-so over my very own sky. Though I'd never found a thing to fuss about concerning the manner in which the real true heavens were decorated, it was a genuine pleasure to do it myself. So, every year, for variety, I switched off where I hung each of our stars, and Daddy would hammer in a nail wherever I asked him to, for the new stars Mama made.

On my way back to fetch another star from the trunk, that last thought stopped me in mid-tiptoe. For, I realized, there wouldn't be even one new star to hang this year. There would never be a new star again.

18

Going Great Guns

I GAVE UP DECORATING, my spirits were too low and too heavy to lug back and forth across the cabin hanging any more stars. I just set down on the chair and stared at the dog. In her sleep, she let out a sigh of contentment, and from inside me came a sigh of my own.

But at the tail end of it, my sigh turned into a giggle. On account of, one minute there lay that still, peaceful dog, and then, right while I was looking at her, why, she started running in her sleep. All four of her big feet took to paddling and jerking like she was chasing after something; I reckoned it might be a rabbit. Or, it could have been the other way around and something was bearing down on *her*. Her eyebrows joined the race; they puckered up and stretched out smooth, then puckered up again. Her nose began to twitch, sniffing and sniffing, and I reckoned it was a rabbit after all.

"Mm . . . mm. Mm," she whined, and on she ran.

Seemed like her feet were picking up speed. I hoped she wasn't going downhill at that rate. Daddy always preached never to go too fast down a slope, for your legs could get away from you, and it made stopping at the proper time uncertain.

Right then, I had to laugh out loud again. That girl gave two muffled little barks through her closed, floppy lips. "Wf. Wf," she said like she truly meant it, and then her eyes popped open wide.

She lifted her head and stared about the room as though she was hunting for the rabbit.

Then her eyes lit on me.

She ambled to her feet and gave a long, two-part stretch. First her front end lengthened out along the floor and her rear end went up, then the hind parts stretched out long while the front parts stood up.

"Owwwwoo," the dog said in a big yawn and, staring straight at me, she shook herself and trotted out the door before I could say a word.

Well, sir, I stared at the empty space where she'd been just half a second before, then I jumped into my coat and snatched down my itchy woolen cap and hightailed it onto the porch.

"Dog!" I swiveled my head side to side so fast I felt dizzy. My eyes were like bright lanterns swinging over the ground, searching her out. Not finding her.

"Dog, come back, come back right now. You hear? Do you hear, dog?"

"Boof." Her voice came from behind the cabin. I stretched over the edge of the porch, trying to peer around the side. I couldn't see hide nor hair of her.

"Do-og," I hollered, and tried to put a lot of enthusiasm into my voice. "Come on now. Come." That last I tried to say real strong and sure.

"Boof," she hollered again, and then, from the opposite side of the cabin from which I was peering, she came bounding by. I caught a glimpse of feet as she loped by; that right front was hitting flat, but keeping up pretty good; her tail was straight up at attention, and then, she was gone behind the cabin again. My heart started to pound, for the only thing I could figure was that she was being chased. A hungry bear, or even a cougar might come round the corner of the cabin any second.

I took a couple steps toward the door, but I couldn't just leave her to get eaten.

"Dog!"

"Boof!"

And there she came again, still going great guns.

"What in the Sam Hill?" I called out as she whisked by.

Three more times that girl circled the cabin, her bum leg swinging wide of her body, but each time she was the lone runner; nobody else ever showed.

At long last, after the final go round, she threw herself down in the snow before me. Her tongue flopped out the side of her mouth; her heavy breaths made little puffs of steam in the wintry cold.

"What got into you?" I squatted down at the edge of the porch, set my elbows on my knees and my chin in my hands, and looked hard at the dog. I wondered if she had the hydrophobia like Daddy had worried, but she wasn't frothing at the mouth or looking crazy.

As a matter of fact, she looked plain cheerful. Why, she was right next door to smiling at me.

It was then that she popped her back end up into the air, and set to wagging her tail like there was no tomorrow.

"Boof," she said, and she pounced her front legs back and forth on the snow and kept abeating the air with that feathered tail of hers.

I shook my head. "I don't know what you're saying. Let's go in to the warm." I stood up, but when I did, that dog hopped her whole self backward.

"Boof."

"All right, but let's go inside, my ears sting." I headed toward the door, and the dog bolted toward me and grabbed the hem of my coat in her teeth and tugged me backward. I turned round, and when I did that, why, she let go and jumped from the porch and ran off a few steps.

"Boof. Boof."

Light was beginning to dawn. I started for the door again, to test my notion, and there she came at a run and set to dragging me backward by my coat. That girl was playing! She wanted a game of chase like Mama and I used to have.

I chased her to the edge of the porch, and she ran a little distance away. When she saw I hadn't followed her like I was supposed to, she tried to encourage me.

"Boof."

Every bit of myself longed to jump down and have a game with her, but I looked at how far away she was, and seized up. I lowered my head and backed toward the door. I worked the toe of my boot in the wolf's head knothole.

"I can't," I said, and I heard my voice low and heavy with shame. "I can't do that; you'll have to come on back here."

She set down on her haunches and cocked her head, trying to gather my meaning.

"I need to go back indoors now," said I.

Her tail wagged back and forth across the snow. I walked toward the door, and my heart lightened considerable when I heard her pad across the porch behind me, dogging my heels. With her long muzzle leading, the dog pushed past me to get inside first, and looking real serious, she set to digging at the floor before the stove.

Honest, seeing that, a soft blanket of relief lay

down over me real gentle-like, for what her actions told me was that she didn't think I was daft for needing to stay put, needing to come on back inside.

And the feeling was mutual; I left the door standing wide, and I stoked that stove up to bursting.

19

Hiawatha?

"DIGGER?" I WAS LYING down beside the dog to try out some more names on her. She was sound asleep before the warm stove, and she hadn't batted an eye with any of my guesses so far.

"Tramper? Lopey? Playful?"

A snore was all she offered.

I thought a while longer.

"Brownie?"

Nothing.

"Girl?"

I stretched my thinking and pondered where she might have come from. That wondering led me over to the bookstand and to a poem Mama had often read me portions of. It was a whole book of a poem by the gentleman Henry Wadsworth Longfellow. I settled back down by the dog and hunted through to the part I wanted to read to her. I lifted one of her floppy ears so she could hear me better.

> *"So he journeyed westward, westward,*
> *Left the fleetest deer behind him,*
> *Left the antelope and bison;*
> *Crossed the rushing Esconaba,*
> *Crossed the mighty Mississippi,*
> *Passed the Mountains of the Prairie,*
> *Passed the land of Crows and Foxes,*
> *Passed the dwellings of the Blackfeet,*
> *Came unto the Rocky Mountains . . . "*

Now, I knew full well the dog wasn't a boy, and I didn't figure her for an Indian, but I whispered the name into her ear anyhow.

"Hiawatha?"

The dog gave her silky ear a twitch so it slipped from my fingers and fell back into place.

"Reckon not," said I, and I just let that sleeping dog

lie and had myself some bread and honey and then worked for a long time at my day's ciphering and spelling.

And the dog, well, that girl just went on napping. She slept and slept, like it had been quite a little while since she'd felt so easy.

Late afternoon shadows slid over the porch and then into the cabin, and evening hunger crept into my stomach, so I set to cutting up vegetables and venison for more stew. Even with the smell of supper cooking, the dog did not wake up. I went so far as to take the lid off the pot and wave the savory aroma directly at her nose, but she just lay there, so very still.

I stood looking down at her slack form, and a daymarish thought came into my head: She was dead. Just like Mama, she had up and died with no struggle. My head started to spin, and my lungs tightened up and only made little grabs at the air. I reached out for the table, for my legs were so trembly, I didn't think they'd hold much longer.

"Dog?" My voice wouldn't do more than whisper.

She didn't answer.

I slid down to my knees and peered through the

dimming light into her face.

"Oh, please, dog. Don't be dead. Don't be dead."

Of a sudden, while we were nose to nose, a vicious growl burst out from deep inside her, and the dog leaped up onto all fours.

"Lordy!" I yelled it out and fell right over backward, I was so startled and my legs so weak from my worry.

The dog didn't give me a second look but jumped over me and charged through the open door, barking loud, loud, sounding the alarm that someone was acoming.

I righted myself and scurried out behind her. It was quite a little minute before my eyes picked up what the dog had already told me. Sure-fire, there was Daddy, just stepping out from the trees onto the clear plain of white. As he trudged forward, I saw that his sled was almost bare again. He was certain to feel even more down in the mouth with a second day of hard luck.

I tried to shush the dog, but she wasn't having it. Just like before, she lunged back and forth across the porch, barking and growling.

Daddy stopped and lifted his head and stood gazing long in the direction of the dog before he started up walking again.

When the dog tried to leap to the far side of the porch, I grabbed her about the neck and held her head firm between my hands and looked her square in the eye.

"This is your last chance to set things right with Daddy. Hush up and behave yourself."

She tried to twist her head away and get back to barking, but I held on. Her brown eyes stretched way over to the side, trying to land Daddy back in their sights.

"I'm serious, dog," I told her. "If you want to keep staying and eating and being warm, you'll have to make friends. That man coming from the woods, that's the gentleman responsible for your recent good fortune."

Her tongue lolled out of her mouth, and she began to pant. I figured that to be from a feeling of frustration from having to sit and listen. That thought sinking in made my heart soften, for I often felt that very same way when I had to stay still and tend to my lessons.

"Please," I said real soft to her. "I want you to stay.

I want it something awful."

That girl looked me in the eye and gave out a tiny whine, and then she set down right next to me and watched Daddy come on.

She sat still enough all right, but as Daddy got closer, a low, steady growl hummed in her throat.

"Hush," I told her, but it didn't make an impression.

When I could see Daddy's face pretty clear, I called out a greeting, but the dog misunderstood and thought I was warning him off.

"Boof!" she hollered, and jumped up. "Boof, boof, boof."

I clamped my hands around her soft muzzle. "Here now. Stop that, dog." I shook my head at her and looked up just in time to see Daddy step onto the porch shaking his own head.

"I see the dog's come back," he shouted over the dog's rumpus.

"Boof. Boof, boof, boof-boof-boof-boof."

"Yes, sir, you were right, Daddy." I cupped my hands around my mouth so the sound would carry, and yelled back to him. "She's been here all day long."

"Boof."

"Reckon you can stop your barking now, dog." Daddy's voice had a little pique to it.

"Boof. Boof-boof."

"Hush. Hush," I told her. "She's protecting our house, Daddy."

"Boof."

"Hmph," Daddy said, and stepped past her into the cabin.

Jackets On

DADDY WAS SURE tolerant about eating dinner with his jacket and hat on. And, he was silent on the subject of the dog growling low all during the meal. Honest, he was silent on all subjects. I reckoned he found it simpler than shouting over the ruckus.

As for herself, the dog quieted down once I served up her own supper. Afterward, she flopped down and got comfortable before the stove's fire.

So, that is to say, everything went slick until bedtime, when Daddy firmed up.

"That door's got to be shut for the night, Dessa Dean."

"Yes, sir, but I think the dog will get all stirred up again if I shut it tight."

"Put her out on the porch."

"Yes, sir, but I believe she's accustomed to the warmth now. I doubt she'll take to sleeping in the cold again."

"Don't matter if she takes to it or not. The dog goes outside, and the door gets closed. Now."

He hadn't left even a bug-sized space for discussion.

The dog followed me out to the porch with no second thoughts, her tail wagging cheerily.

I cupped her head in my hands and looked her in the eye.

"You're to spend the night on the porch, dog. Over there, where you have before, in your lay. Then, in the morning, once Daddy sets out, you can come in and warm up and have some food. So, stay right here now, and I'll see you first thing tomorrow." I gave her a reassuring nod, and a hug around the neck, and before I shut the door against the cold, I filled up my eyes with the sight of her. There she sat, her head cocked, watching me in a patient manner.

Seemed like, as I slipped beneath the pile of quilts on my cot, that everything was settled.

And so it was, for a time.

Came a scratching at the door.

Came a whine from out there, too.

"Dessa Dean, get that dog quiet."

"Yes, sir." I hopped out of bed and ran for the door. I didn't even make note of the number of steps involved.

I creaked the door open and stepped out into winter.

"Ra." The dog gave a quiet little bark of greeting.

"I missed you, too, dog," I whispered to her, and ran my warm hand over her chilled coat. In the cold dark I knelt down beside her and slipped my arm around her neck, tucked my nose behind her floppy ear.

"I'm sorry to say it, but you have to stay out here for the duration of the night. And you have to be quiet about it. That's important, dog."

"Mmmm."

It was just a little whine she gave out, but, oh, it weighed heavy on my heart.

"Well, let's think on it for a moment." I said that to

be encouraging. "Tell you what, dog, I'll just see about getting a little bite for you, to help you sleep. Sometimes, if my stomach isn't quite filled, it distracts me so I can't settle down. Could be we're just alike that way. You'll have to eat quick so as not to draw any varmints, though. Wait right here."

I stepped back inside and closed the door as quiet as I could.

"Mmm."

"Shh!" I tried to whisper soft enough not to vex Daddy and loud enough to hush the dog. Both of them were quiet, so it worked.

First off, I rummaged around on my hands and knees till I found my socks over by my cot, for my toes felt like they were pretty near turned to icicles. Then, I felt around for the dog's bowl and tiptoed it over to the storage bin and scrounged for another potato. Honest, I felt a little bit of worry, for it seemed like I was going against the dog's nature by keeping on giving her vegetables and suchlike.

Out to the porch I tiptoed and plunked the bowl down before the dog.

"There you go."

Real ladylike, she plucked the tater out of the bowl with her teeth and, holding it steady with her front feet, commenced to gnaw on it. Seemed like vegetables were fine with her.

"Sleep tight," said I, and gave her a kiss on top of her wide head. Then I scurried back inside before she could get distracted from her midnight snack or set to thinking about being all alone in the dark.

Under my mountain of quilts I crawled, and pretty soon, I was warm as toast again, and pretty soon after that, I was sound asleep.

21

Shahrazad!

"MM. MM. RA."

Those were the next sounds I heard, and the next thing I felt was a cold, wet nose on my own. After the nose came a nuzzling under my hand, and a soft, broad head.

A smile spread through my whole self.

"Mmm. Mm."

I sat up on my cot, and let my sleepy eyes soak up the dog in the light of day.

"Soon as I had the door open a crack, she barged right in."

Daddy's voice had a little edge, but his eyes were smiling.

"She's figured out where to get fed and where to get warm, looks like." He stood before the cutting board, slicing bacon.

"Yes, sir. She's real smart," said I.

"I been watching her stroll around the last little while," he said. "Appears to me she's putting a tad more weight on that foot than she was just the other day, and that whole leg seems to be coming into alignment. I reckon that tendon only got a bad bruise and is starting to heal with her able to rest it like she's been. Next few days will tell." He turned back to keep track of his slicing.

"How would that have happened, Daddy?"

"I've seen it before. In coyotes. Not so uncommon."

Daddy scooped up the thick bacon strips and carried them over to the stovetop, where the skillet was heating up. Soon as he turned in our direction, the dog began her low, humming growl. Daddy gave her a frown and laid out the slices one next to the other in the cast-iron frying pan.

I gave her a shake of my head and, pretending she hadn't said a thing, I spoke up just a mite louder.

"But, how, Daddy? How would the bruising happen?"

Mama often said getting answers from Daddy was like trying to get blood from a turnip.

"Coulda been a log. Coulda been a stone."

Slowly, he flipped each slice over with a fork and pressed it down in the skillet so it sizzled and spit.

"But, *how*, Daddy? How would it actually happen?"

Other times, Mama said getting Daddy's answers was like squeezing water from a stone.

"Oh. Well, Dessa Dean." He said that part so innocent-like, as though he was just that moment catching on to what my question was. "That's a cinch. A critter chasing or getting chased is legging it as fast as it can, and once in a while, a foot lands wrong in trying to jump a log, or scrambling over a rocky patch of ground."

Daddy speared the bacon one strip at a time with the fork, shook the grease off it into the skillet, and laid it all out on a clean plate.

"So, landing crooked is what makes the bruise happen?"

Sometimes Mama would phrase her sentiment like this: "John, you're as tight with words as a miser is with his money."

"It's the fact of not landing square on the paw, but

further up the leg, on the ankle, so it smacks on a rock or a log," he said. "The blow bruises the tendon; it swells up, stays weak for a time."

"And that would have made her whole entire leg go cock-eyed like it is?"

"If the critter don't lay down and rest, and no wild animal that's got to provide for itself is going to take it easy and wait to heal, the injury down low starts to affect everything up the line."

"You reckon that's the case with the dog, Daddy?"

"I reckon."

And just like that, the conversation ended, like Daddy had run himself out of words. We finished our breakfast with just chewing noises and a low growl from the dog to fill the empty air spaces. When Daddy pushed his chair back from the table, she stood up, too, and raised her hackles. Daddy just shook his head and looked disgusted at her.

"I better trap a coon or a muskrat, something good to eat, pretty soon, or that dog's liable to be going hungry again. We're getting down to bone on the deer carcass, and the crik flow hasn't gotten strong enough to melt out the deep pools to allow for any fishing."

Daddy stepped outside with nary a thought to leaving the door cracked for the dog. I had just a split-second glimpse of him tramping through the snow toward the shed to carve the day's meat, and then the dog let out a panicky yelp and dashed at the closed door. Up she jumped on her hind legs, and when she came down, her claws ascratching on it all the way to the bottom, she started in pacing and digging at its lower edge and whining and barking, just as she had the day before.

Well, sir, I hightailed it over, took another quick glance out the window to see Daddy turn and gaze toward the cabin, and then I nudged the dog out of the way quick as I could, for I didn't want to see her hurt her poor nose again or a paw, nor any other part. Soon as I got the door cracked, she gave me a scolding.

"Boof!" is what she said, and followed it up with a little growl to say I should have known better than to let it happen.

"I apologize," said I.

And that was the end of it.

Daddy was silent in a wintry sort of way when he brought the meat in, and silent when he lugged in three armloads of wood and stacked it log by log next to the stove. He had a long, hard stare for the dog when he finished; it was certain he'd heard the racket she made.

But just before Daddy set out for his traps, he softened up a mite and smiled into my eyes and gave a little nod around the cabin.

"You did a fine decorating job, Dessa Dean. Everything's mighty dolled up. Looks right Christmasy." And out from the cabin he stepped, leaving the door ajar.

I turned and smiled at the dog.

She thumped her tail on the floor.

"Look here, girl." I crossed over to the Advent calendar. "This is the twenty-second day of the month of December. It's the second day of your return." I pulled a brown corduroy camel from the pocket embroidered with the number twenty-two and held it out for the dog to see.

She pressed her wet nose to the corduroy and gave it a good going over with her sniffer. Then she cocked her head at me as if to ask why I was awasting her time on something that didn't smell the least little bit like food.

"It's a beast of the desert," I explained. "You can ride on them if there's no horses close at hand. Strange-looking, aren't they, with those big lumps on their backs. This one that Mama sewed, it's a one-humper, but they come with two humps, as well. Deserts have critters a lot different from what we're used to around here, girl. Why, there's no bears nor geese nor chipmunks to speak of in the desert. What there are, are camels, like I said, and there's magical creatures, too, called jinns."

"Ra," she said, like she'd heard of them before, but I doubted it.

"A jinni is a kind of man that can turn to smoke and live inside a brass lamp only this big." I showed her with my hands. "A jinni has great powers and not much liking for normal people; it's a bad combination."

I snapped the corduroy camel up right behind the first one so a caravan commenced to form on the calendar's red felt background.

"Come over here, dog. There's something I want to show you." I went over to the bookstand and set down before it, my legs crossed Indian-fashion, and the dog settled next to me, her legs just out regular.

"This is a secret hiding place of Mama's and mine," I told her. "Now I'm going to share it with you."

I tugged the tattered, gray dictionary from the bottom shelf and let it thump to the floor. Then I bent over and peered into the dark space where it had set, and reached my hand way back in there. A smile stretched my lips when my fingers brushed the cool leather cover of a book tucked up sideways against the back wall of the bookstand.

"There's a special book way back in there, dog, full of stories from the desert. And all of them, all the stories are told by a fine lady named Miss Shahrazad. You know why she bothered telling all these stories, dog? To keep the sultan occupied so he wouldn't chop off her head. Can you imagine? Some of the stories, though, go just a mite beyond exciting. Honest, they can give you gooseflesh, especially if you read them after sundown. The stories about the jinn always alarmed me the very most, and Mama, to be certain I wouldn't have nightmares, why, she'd stow the book way back there when we were through with it, behind the heavy old dictionary. 'Out of sight, out of mind,' is what she'd say, and it worked every time. I never had a bad dream about the terrible jinni so long as the book was way in the back of the bookstand. How 'bout that, dog?"

She thumped her tail.

"Still, do you know? If I was down in the dumps, or feeling punk with a fever, there wasn't another book in the wide world that could take my mind off my troubles half so well as . . ."

And I pulled out the small, plump book and held it up so the dog could see the front cover with its fancy, gold lettering.

"*The Arabian Nights*!"

"Ra!"

Around on my sitter I spun myself, still with my legs folded, and leaned back against the bookshelves. I patted my leg, and the dog lifted her head so her chin rested on my thigh. The first few pages of the book I just leafed through, for they said all the things I had already related to the dog about the oh-so-clever Shahrazad.

"This first story is called 'The Fisherman and the Jinni,' I told her. "Don't be scared, now, dog, I'm right here."

She sighed and closed her eyes, and I began to read out loud.

Honest, I'm not certain entirely how much of the story she heard, for she started in snoring pretty quick, but I kept right on, for it had been ever so long a time since Mama had read from the book to me. And, the feel of the book in my hands, the sound of the words in the air, well, somehow those things made me feel happy and sad all at one and the same time. I couldn't quit the story till I got to the very end.

When I had read the last word, I hugged the book tight, and after a little minute I realized my cheeks were wet with tears from missing Mama, and where they'd dripped from my jawbone, they'd landed on the dog's head and made a damp spot.

I rubbed my cheeks with the backs of my hands and petted the dark brown wet spot on the dog's head till it dried and turned back to medium brown, and I concentrated hard on the little corner of peace the dog snoozing on my leg provided me. Then I pushed my thoughts in a different direction.

Shahrazad seemed still to be drifting through my mind; so I thought on how brave she was. Even though she knew that sultan was cutting off his wives' heads left and right, a new one every day on account of being mad at his first original wife, why, Shahrazad insisted on signing up to be his next wife. And then, didn't she keep him so busy with story after story for one thousand and one nights that he ended up with such a fondness for her that she was able to take a break from all the story-telling. Yes, sir, a smart, smart lady was Miss Shahrazad.

"Shahrazad." I whispered the name so I wouldn't wake the dog. It had a beautiful sound to it. "Shahrazad." I looked down at the dog. "Shahrazad." Her ear twitched. Could it be? "Shahrazad." Now I knew the dog wasn't any more familiar with sultans or jinns or desert life than she was with Indians, but I had come up empty trying names that resembled the dog, such as Brownie and Ruff and Snowflake and Blizzard, and I'd fallen flat with Hiawatha, trying to tie in the dog's rambling nature, and I'd found no pur-chase in naming her for the way she acted, like Playful.

Mayhap she was set on a name that sounded beau-tiful when it was out in the air.

"Shahrazad," I whispered, and then lifted the dog's floppy ear and whispered it again. "Shahrazad."

Even though the dog lifted her hind leg and scratched her ear back into place and let out a deep sigh and went directly back to snoring, I didn't feel discouraged about the name. No, sir, I felt sure I'd hit on the real thing.

22

Burdensome Words

WHEN THE DOG awoke, she gave a long, lazy stretch at both ends and asked politely to go outside. I obliged and watched her trot behind the cabin. Stoking the stove was next on my mind, for even though the sun was shining bright, the air was mighty cold with that door cracked.

"Ra," the dog called from outside.

I finished up with the wood and pulled my itchy woolen cap down, slipped on my coat, and stepped out to the porch.

"Ra."

She was wanting some play time; her front end was

down, her rear end was up, and her tail was wagging like crazy.

"I told you, Shahrazad, I can't get off the porch. I just really can't. I'm sorry."

There I was again, feeling bad about the way things stood with me.

The dog set back on her haunches and cocked her head at me.

"Roo," she said in a hopeful tone, her muzzle up in the air.

I set down on the icy wooden planks and dropped my chin and held real still for quite a little minute, the crown of my head warming under the touch of the winter sun, the whispery winter breeze causing my forehead and cheeks to stiffen and numb up. Far off in a juniper stand a crow cawed, and from the pale, bare branches of the nearby scrub oak came the slow, tickly rhythm of icicles letting go cold drops of water, and my skin prickled to the noise.

The whole world was going on around me, and I filled up with such a want to run lickety-split into it all and not be scared, to give a holler 'cause I was so happy being in the goings-on of the world, instead of a holler caused by a daymare, well, it was like all of a sudden turning into a thin sheet of ice on Willow Creek that a deer had just stepped upon. Any second, any second I wouldn't be able to bear the pressure anymore, and the fragile ice of me would crack and splinter into a million, billion pieces.

And then something dropped into my lap. It was a pinecone, put there by Shahrazad. She was smiling at me and wagging.

"Ra!"

"What?"

"Ra."

She sounded a tad impatient.

"I don't understand. I don't know what you want. It's a pinecone."

Gently, just like she had with the midnight tater, she picked the pinecone up with her teeth and dropped it on the porch planks before me.

"Ra."

The dog lowered her front end and raised her back parts and wagged so hard her tail made a whooshing sound in the air.

I knew she was trying to teach me a new game, and

I felt embarrassed that I didn't understand what I was to do.

I looked at her and shrugged and shook my head.

The dog, once again, real dainty-like, picked the pinecone up in her teeth and dropped it back in my lap.

"Ra!"

And she did a backward pounce.

"Oh!" I finally understood what she was trying to tell me. "All right."

I picked the pinecone up and drawing my throwing arm back as far as I could, I pitched it away out into the un-tracked-on snow; and sure enough, the dog skittered across the porch and leaped into the air and bounded after that rascal pinecone and wrestled it till it gave up.

Back she brought it and dropped it in my lap once more.

"Ra!"

I laughed right out loud, I felt so happy.

"Ra!"

I wound up my throwing arm and threw that pinecone again, far, far as I could.

And then, when she brought it back to me, I threw it again,

and again,

and again.

My muscles got to where they were good and worn out, and finally I said, "Shahrazad, let's go on inside now. I'm frozen, and I can't lift my arms even one more time."

She stared at me from out in the snow.

"Shahrazad."

The dog turned, ignoring me fully, and trotted behind the cabin.

I felt a little doubt creep into my heart. "But, it's such a beautiful name," I called to her.

I set the pinecone next the door and went on inside, leaving it cracked for you-know-who, then I stoked up the belly of the stove again and backed up close to it to warm my parts.

The dog came wagging in a few minutes later, her muzzle covered in snow from snuffling through it.

"Shahrazad," I said to her.

She didn't even have a look for me, just went to the stove, started in digging at the floor, and flopped down and began another nap.

For a while, I just set in one of the table chairs, and

every few minutes I'd call out, "Shahrazad," for I so wanted that to be her name. Honest, though, I did not get a word or an open eye, or even an ear twitch in response. It was discouraging.

Pretty soon it turned out I'd wasted so much time trying to talk her into the name that the day's light was dimming. It was time to get supper.

When Daddy arrived home, everything happened like the previous day. Except that the dog's barking and growling, and having to keep his jacket on to stay warm seemed to make Daddy a good sight grumpier than it all had the day before.

Luck had still been poor in his traps, too, but he had brought home two scrawny squirrels he'd shot that I could cook up the next day after I'd picked the bird-shot out of them. Neither one of us favored squirrel, though their skins made fine little pouches to store small trinkets or garden seeds.

I served up the dog's food quick as I could so she would hush up, and when I set our food plates down on the table, I made a try at conversation, hoping to give Daddy something to think about other than empty traps and stringy squirrel meat.

"I can't seem to strike on the right name for the dog, Daddy."

"Hmph" was all he offered.

"I've tried all manner of names; she doesn't seem to take to any of them."

Daddy stuck a chunk of turnip in his mouth.

"I've tried Brownie, and she didn't answer to that. I tried Playful, but she didn't recognize that one, either. Then, I tried Hiawatha."

"Hiawatha? Where'd you get that notion from?"

I felt encouraged to go on from Daddy's display of interest.

"On account of how she's traveled around. Like in the poem Mama used to read: 'So he journeyed westward, westward, / Left the fleetest deer behind him' . . . I can't say the rest without looking at the book. Do you want me to get the book, Daddy?"

"No need," he said.

I stuck a bit of turnip in my own mouth and just chewed for a minute to give Daddy time to put out some words if he wanted.

He didn't seem inclined.

"Today, I thought sure I'd struck on the right name

for her: Shahrazad."

"Never heard of that."

"It's from a book Mama and I used to read. About a lady in a far-off desert."

"Hmph. Don't reckon a dog born and bred in this part of the world would appreciate being called something like that. Shard, Shradza," his tongue tangled in the fancy, silky, sandy desert sounds.

"Shahrazad," I corrected. "I guess she didn't take to it. But I've tried everything else I could think of."

"The dog'll let you know when you hit on the right one."

"You mean she'll tell me what her true name is?" My voice squeaked I was so excited by the thought. "How? How will she tell me, Daddy? What will she do?"

"Can't say exactly how or what, but she'll let you know when you get it right."

"How do you know?" I prodded. "Daddy?"

"What schoolwork did you do today?"

And just like that, there was no more discussion of the dog's name. Instead, I had to fess up that I had gotten precious little accomplished on my studies the whole day, and when Daddy asked, I had to likewise admit I still hadn't come up with a twelve-times-twelve problem.

Daddy's look was stiff, like his face had been out in the winter air for too long a time. I reckoned my studies weren't the only thing making him look so; there had been plenty of times Mama told me how hard it was for Daddy to provide sufficient food day in and day out to feed us and how that wore on a body. But whatever all the things causing his consternation at that moment, his eyes didn't blink, and his lips stayed set.

And it all caused me to feel smallish and uneasy.

"Dessa Dean," Daddy said low and growly, "that dog is eating us out of house and home, it's burning through logs like there's no tomorrow, the dad-blamed thing is keeping me up at night, and now it's keeping you from your most serious responsibilities. I believe she's doing more harm than good."

Daddy leaned even closer across the table and locked his eyes straight into mine so I couldn't quit staring back even though I very much wanted to. I longed for Mama to step over from the stove and say something such as, "Now, John, don't go making a mountain out of a molehill."

And then, while Daddy's eyes were burning into mine, my ears picked up the dog starting to growl from across the room. I heard her creep toward me, her growl growing louder as she got closer. She stood beside me. I reached out for her and laid my hand on her back; her hackles were standing straight. She was protecting me, sure.

At that moment, I looked right back at Daddy, and now it was because I wanted to, not because I had to. And even though there was nothing in the wide world I wanted to talk about less, I made myself say the words, for there was one thing I was set on hanging on to no matter what, namely, the dog.

Whatever her name was.

I took a deep breath and hunched my shoulders up tight.

"Well, one thing is sure," said I. "My ears haven't been gripping me near so much, and I haven't been plagued by even one nightmare or a single daymare since the dog came to be my friend. And that's something, Daddy. It's something for me, at least."

And those words I spoke made me shake all over,

but I didn't look away until after Daddy had dropped his own eyes off of mine. Before they fell, I saw them fill up with something, something that made me swallow hard. And I knew it to be that prickly, uncomfortable mix of happy and sad feelings going on at one and the same time in a body.

In the quiet, with no more words coming from me, and only the whistle of a heavy sigh leaking out from Daddy, I took note that the dog had stopped her low, humming growl. The only sound beside the pop of wood in the stove, was the mournful wind arattling the windowpanes.

But then I heard something that made the breath catch in my throat and sent a hot burn into my cheeks.

"Dessa Dean, I apologize."

Why, I felt just as unsettled as I would if I'd been taken by a daymare. There was Daddy, in his regular gruff voice, saying words that I had never known to pass his lips ever before, and I was the one who had caused him to say them.

My next words tumbled all over each other trying to get out, and they fell pell-mell and shrill into the stove-warmed air.

"Oh, no! You don't have to say that. You don't have to at all."

Well, sir, Daddy leaped out of his chair like he'd been hit with buckshot, and rushed toward me and grabbed my arms, which hung at my sides.

The dog stepped closer to me and showed her teeth to Daddy, but he plain ignored her and kneeled down before me, and we were of the same size.

It seemed my hearing sort of shut off then; there were more of Daddy's words buzzing in the air, but I couldn't sort them out. The only thing I knew was that he was clutching me to him, and while that caused the biggest ache way deep in my heart, I also felt washed clean, like a shirt rubbed on stones in Willow Creek on Mama's washing day. Which was always Thursday.

23

Sharing

DADDY DIDN'T ACT like himself the rest of the night, and it made me feel squirmy, honest. I sent the dog straight out onto the porch to sleep when Daddy first said it was time to go to roost, and I crawled under my quilts in a hurry. I was most anxious to put an end to the day.

But, the dog had a different thought. The barest few minutes had passed until she commenced whining something fierce. Her voice mixed with the howl of the wind; and between the two complaints, things were plain clamorous in the cabin.

Daddy didn't utter a single word or even let go a heavy sigh, but I knew good and well there was slight chance he was sleeping through that racket.

I lay still and bunched up for a time, hoping the dog would settle, but her whining grew ever louder till it rose above the wind. So out of bed I crept and dished up a carrot and carried her bowl out to the porch. Dainty, dainty she plucked the carrot from the dish, and I sneaked back to my cot.

Even before I'd warmed up fully, her whining started up again and before very long, it became a high-pitched howl.

Only thing I could figure was the poor girl was suffering in the cold, for the wind was still whipping the snow and shrieking and punching things in the dark night. It was enough to make even a fattened-up bear shiver, I reckoned.

Quick like a bunny I snatched the top quilt off my cot and lugged it out to the porch. I could make out the dog curled tight in her icy lay, so I shuffled up to her and spread the quilt out over her entire self and tucked it in around the edges, and pulled it over the top part of her head so her eyes and nose were all that stuck out into the cold.

"Go to sleep, girl," I told her. "This isn't a night to

make a ruckus, really it isn't."

And I hustled back inside.

That did the trick. I slept through the rest of the dark hours, and, so far as I knew, Daddy and the dog did, too.

When my eyelids rolled up in the morning that girl was pulled up next to my cot, nudging her muzzle under my arm, and Daddy had already set out. Soft light filled up the cabin in a slow, creeping manner, as if it was feeling its way into all the corners. Mama's Christmas stars were beginning to reflect the sun, and fancy patches and strips of light danced a jig on the walls.

I smiled as I set up, taking in all the flickering patterns and shapes.

The dog turned her head to follow my gaze, and when she caught sight of the lights jumping across the wall, she cocked her head in wonderment, and trotted over for a closer look.

It made me laugh outright, to see her press her nose to all the little light squiggles on the wall that she could reach, trying to figure them out. Even sniffing as hard as she could didn't tell her what she wanted to know, so she stood up on her hind legs and barked at the high ones.

"It's light from Mama's Christmas stars. Makes you feel happy just looking, doesn't it, girl."

I threw off my pile of quilts and went straight over to the Advent calendar. The dog gave up on the dancing lights and padded over next to me.

"Today is December the twenty-third," I told her, "and that marks the third day of your return."

Out from pocket twenty-three, I eased an angel and held her out for the dog to sniff her puffy, cottony self.

"My mama's an angel now, dog."

I hadn't meant to say that, but the truth was, after the way in which the dog had stood up for me the night past, and how early-morning-drowsy I still was, why, I felt easy enough to show her something of my heart. My words were low and whispery, though, for even though I wanted the dog to know, I didn't want to hear the words too loud.

I snapped the angel onto the red felt next to her sisters from pockets nine and fifteen so they made a Heavenly trio, and then I looked down into the dog's brown eyes.

"Come here, girl," I said. "There's something else I want to show you."

And she padded behind me over to where the carved angel set. Gently, oh, so, I cupped my hands around the angel and traced her high cheekbones with my finger. I scooped her up and presented her to the dog.

"This is what my mama looks—looked like, dog. It's the closest I have to a picture of her. Daddy carved it." And that made me think to say, "That's one more reason you shouldn't growl at him."

She seemed to understand that it was a precious and delicate thing I was sharing with her, for when I held the lovely angel out, the dog didn't prod her with her nose, did not snuffle her all over searching for a food scent, but softly, lightly, touched her scraped brown nose to the beautiful, perfect wood, and the while long, the dog held my gaze.

I turned my own eyes back to the angel.

"I wasn't daft at all, before Mama died." I tried to say it like I was saying it just to myself, but, honest, I knew the dog was listening hard and taking my words in. "I never had a daymare my whole life long before Mama froze. Losing Mama is what made my ears start to torment me and what stuck me in the house."

After that, I had courage to look back at her.

"I believe it's a similar thing with your leg. Mayhap the part of you that doesn't work quite right has something to do with your dislike of close spaces. Like my ears and me not being able to tolerate the wide world anymore."

I smiled down at her and rubbed the water out of my eyes so the dog stopped looking blurry, and I reached out, stroking her big ol' head.

The dog was done with sad feelings, though.

"Ra," she said, and headed across the cabin, nudged the door wide with her nose and trotted out.

I tugged my itchy woolen cap down a mite further and hauled the chamber pot out from beneath my cot.

For breakfast, I allowed the dog one-half of a skillet-warmed squirrel, after I'd got all the birdshot out so she wouldn't crack a tooth, and I stretched the meal with chunks of taters and turnips. When the squirrel aroma drifted outside, it wasn't but the blink of an eye before the dog came skittering through the door.

She set down practically on my feet and pointed her muzzle into the air.

"Rrooo!"

I smiled, thinking on how she said that very same thing whenever she was wound up about something.

That girl was mighty hungry and didn't need convincing to tend to business when I set the bowl in front of her.

For myself, I preferred the regular bread and honey to start my day; so after I'd washed my hands and face, I slathered up a slice and washed it down with some cold water, and then, so there wouldn't be a chance of anything unsettling happening with Daddy *that* evening, I set to my day's work like a plow horse with blinders on.

The dog had a different idea. She wanted to play and let me know it by nudging at my leg with her long, brown nose.

I ignored her the first time.

And the second.

She gave my leg another good bump and then set back on her haunches and let out a little growl.

Honest, I had to smile, but I stayed firm.

"I can't play right now, dog. I've got to tend to this schoolwork, or we'll both be in trouble when Daddy gets home."

She seemed to understand, for without another word, she walked outside.

Well, sir, after two long hours of concentrating on my history reading and writing on my history lesson, my brain and my hand needed a rest, so I put on my coat and went in search of the dog.

Turned out, all I had to do to find her was step onto the porch. She was curled in her lay, gnawing on a pinecone. Or rather, she was gnawing on a whole load of pinecones. Truth be told, she was surrounded by them. Apparently, while I was thinking about Emperor Constantine of the Holy Roman Empire, that girl was occupying herself by gathering all the pinecones anywhere close by.

I smiled at her.

"Fetch?" I asked.

"Ra," she said, and gave one of her luxurious two-part stretches and wagged at me.

I picked up one of the pinecones and pitched it away as far as I could toward the canyon.

The dog gave chase, and watching her, I realized that I'd gotten so used to that daft leg of hers that I hardly noticed anymore how it swung out loose and wide away from her body. She was used to it, too. That girl could run like crazy even with the injury. If it hadn't been for that daft leg, she probably never would have come to the cabin.

My next thought shot a tingle of surprise down the back of my neck. *If it wasn't for my ears, I might not have been here to meet her even if she had come.*

The Dad-Blamed Mouse

THERE CAME THE dog, trotting toward me, smiling around the pinecone in her teeth and wagging her tail to beat the band.

I couldn't help but smile myself.

"Come on, girl. Bring it here."

Out to her left, though, something caught her eye, and she stopped stone-still and let the pinecone fall into the snow.

Down to her belly she dropped and commenced to crawl, just as she had her first time in the cabin. Out across the crusty white she crept, inching her way toward a straggly clump of yellowed grass that poked above the snow.

"Come on, girl," I called. "Over here."

But her ears didn't even give a twitch my direction. She was concentrating something fierce.

"What in the Sam Hill?"

I tiptoed out to the edge of the porch until my boot toes dangled in the air, and I squinted my eyes out over the snow, trying to make out something of interest besides that dead grass.

Honest, I didn't see a dad-blamed thing, and I told her as much.

"I don't see a dad-blamed thing but grass, dog. That's nothing to creep around about or try to sneak up on. It's grass. Let's get on back to our game."

I tossed another pinecone her way. It plopped next to her right front leg.

She stopped moving, and I thought I'd convinced her.

But that girl wasn't paying attention to my voice or the pinecone. Not one whit. She had stopped bare inches from the clumpy grass and now slowly, she pulled her hindquarters in under her and didn't move again. She just held like that and stared at the dad-blamed grass.

I shook my head and called out, "All right. We'll just set, if that's all you want to do. We'll just set."

I squatted down on the porch planks and rested my elbows on my knees and my chin in my hands.

A goose winged over us high, high in the air and let out a lonely sounding honk.

The dog didn't take notice.

Some quiet passed, and then a late-day breeze came sighing through the tops of the pines, making the needles on their branches rustle like corduroy trousers.

But the dog did not look up.

She did not prick her ears.

I called out to her again, and a squirrel joined in achattering, achattering. And then, why, the nervy varmint gave a leap and raced across the snow right before the dog and on up a pine onto its lowest branch. There, it fixed its black eye on the dog, and in a loud voice, poked fun at her for not chasing after him like she ought.

Not a muscle twitched in that girl.

Not one.

She just stayed still like a statue, looking all pinched with her hind legs hunched under her.

And then, just as I was about to complain to her again, quicker than the blink of an eye, that dog moved.

Into the air she sprang from her crouched position, her big back feet lifted slightly off the ground as her front end lurched up and forward, and her front feet pounced down hard on the ground.

One split second was all that passed, and the dog looked up at me, smiling around something new that she held between her teeth. As she trotted toward me, grinning and wagging, I saw a little damp spot on her chin. It was blood. The dog was able to hunt again.

A stone of dread plunked into my stomach when I realized what that meant. Why, if she was able to provide for herself once more, she wouldn't need me. She could just pull up stakes and move on, and there I'd be, stuck on the porch forever. Alone.

I set there frozen in that thought for a good long minute, staring at the dog loping toward me.

She looked so pleased with herself, and seeing that, shame began to push the dread out of its way and settle itself in my belly. Shame, realizing what I'd hoped deep in my heart was that the dog wouldn't ever be able to take care of herself again, just so I could have her company. Shame at what a terrible thing it was that I had been ahoping.

Onto the porch she bounded, her muzzle sticky-orange with blood, and right before me she landed. The dog dropped her head and let go the critter from her mouth, and a little dead mouse plopped onto the top of my right boot.

She set down on her haunches, still with the biggest smile on her face, and beat her tail on the wood planks. She tipped her nose straight into the air.

"Rrooo!"

"Well, sir," I said, "that's big news, dog. This means you're fit again. Fit as a fiddle, I reckon. That leg's not holding you back any longer."

I tugged my itchy woolen cap down hard.

"It's big news, all right."

I put sincere effort into sounding happy, trying to feel happy, for that girl was mighty proud and excited with what she'd done.

I gave my boot a little shake to get the mouse off and then bent down and gave the dog a tight hug around the neck.

"That was a real good job, girl," I told her. "I'm proud of you. Reckon the mouse is yours to eat, now that you've shown it to me."

I picked up the floppy, little gray carcass and held it out to her.

Once more she tilted her stained muzzle into the air.

"Roooo."

And that one word told me how excited she was being out in the world and accomplishing what she had.

I kept watching her, and real ladylike, she plucked the mouse from my hand with her choppers and carried it over to her lay. Down she sat, her trophy between her teeth and commenced to crunch it up.

A Saving

"THE DOG IS BACK to hunting for herself, Daddy."

It was my fourth try at conversation at the dinner table that night. Although I had found it mighty encouraging that the dog had neither growled nor barked when he got home but just scowled at him with her ears pulled down and back, Daddy hadn't been interested in discussing it. Nor had he found the dog's new hobby of collecting pinecones comment worthy. Same for Emperor Constantine becoming a Christian man.

But the dog catching her own food weighed heavy on my mind, so I tried again.

"She caught a mouse today. She waited on it for the longest time, so patient. And when it popped out of its hole, why, she pounced on it quick as lightning; it was amazing."

"Hmph."

Daddy'd come up niggardly nil in his traps again. I reckoned it was worrying him in heart and mind.

"I'm scared she might move on, if she's able to provide for herself."

"Could be."

"I've been thinking, Daddy, how to let her know how much I hope she won't go, how much I want for her to stay on."

"Dog's going to do what she's going to do, Dessa Dean."

"But, what I was wanting was to give her something special for Christmas."

"Don't reckon dogs know one day from another."

"Still, what I want is for her to feel like she's a part of the family. So, I'd like for her to have a gift on Christmas Day. I'd like to have one of the heavy leg bones from the deer, Daddy, to give her. I'd like to baste it up with gravy and let it soak in and dry and then give it to her."

"I expect we'll all be agnawing bones for Christmas dinner, lest my luck changes mighty quick or the weather stays warmer long enough so the crik flow melts out the fishing holes."

Daddy shoved his chair back and stood up and blew out the flame of the kerosene lamp.

"I'm going to bed. Put the dog out."

And wouldn't you know it, one more night where it was important that she just hush up and settle down and show Daddy how well behaved a dog she could be, why, instead she set to crying right off.

I tried a bowl of vegetables.

She kept awhining.

I tucked her in snug with a quilt.

She commenced to howl.

I could almost hear Daddy thinking how he hoped the dog *would* go on her way.

I was desperate to hush her up.

So, I pulled on my socks, pulled down my cap, tip-toed twelve bitty steps to my table chair where my coat was, slid it on, went back to my cot for my britches and stuck my cold legs into their cold legs. Then I glumped up the final three of my quilts into my arms and tip-toed to the door.

I creaked it open a mite and peeked out. Cold air bit my nose.

The dog was setting up, her long nose pointed toward me, the quilt still draped over her back.

"Dog? I'm gonna sleep right here next the door. I'll be right here the whole night, so you can rest easy. Hush now and go to sleep."

And with that, the dog curled up tight, hiding her nose beneath her warm tail. She let out a deep sigh and didn't say another word.

I eased the door closed and hunkered down under my quilts. No matter how I piled covers under or over me, I stayed half froze the entire night long.

Long about gray dawn I finally drifted off, and no sooner had I, than Daddy's voice roused me.

"What in the Sam Hill, Dessa Dean?"

I was too cold and tired to offer much in the way of a response; I just scooped up all the quilts again and shuffled them back to my cot and tossed them down and wriggled underneath of them and fell back asleep.

When finally I awoke, it was late in the morning;

only a few of Mama's Christmas stars were still casting dancing lights. But even that little bit made me feel glad. I stretched my arms to get the sleep out of them, and when I lowered them back to the quilt, why, my hands got a surprise.

They came to rest on something warm and wet and sticky. I couldn't imagine, and when I held them up for a look, they were red with blood. I let out a holler that brought the dog trotting from before the stove. I stared at my bloody hands while I threw back the quilts and scrambled off the cot, trying to figure what, and nothing was coming to me.

The dog gave one of my palms a lick, cleaning off a stripe of the blood, and then she nosed under the top quilt where I'd tossed it off. She stuck her whole head in between the folded halves, and when she came out, why, there was a fine dead rabbit in her mouth. A big one. And just as she had the day before with the mouse, she dropped the carcass gently onto my feet.

A wide smile claimed my face.

"Why, dog, I believe you just saved Christmas dinner."

Christmas Eve Comes

"Y OUR NAME HUNTER, by any chance?" I asked the dog while I was washing my hands after skinning and gutting the rabbit, and she was chewing on the ears I'd let her have.

She didn't look up.

"How long you going to keep your name secret from me?"

Still nothing.

"You know all those pinecones you collected yesterday? I have an idea what we could use them for."

With her concentrating on the crunchy rabbit ears and ignoring me, I went and carted in the pinecones and scattered them on the table. Then, I fetched Mama's scrap box.

"I thought I remembered right."

From out the box I pulled a long strand of red plaid ribbon and cut it into sections with Mama's pinking shears. Around the top of all but one pinecone, I knotted the center of the ribbon piece and then tied the ends together so it made a loop. And all around the cabin I went, hanging Christmas pinecones from the backs of the chairs, on the door latch, from the knobs of the cupboards, and then I stood back and looked.

They looked like little Christmas presents. Little Christmas presents from the woods. They were beautiful.

I smiled inside, thinking how even though there wouldn't be any more tin-can stars, still, with the dog's help, we had something new and beautiful for our Christmas.

"Thank you, dog," I said.

I could hardly wait for Daddy to come on home to show him the new decorations and the Christmas dinner the dog had provided. My composition on Emperor Constantine had been the last of my schoolwork for the week, so I was able to spend most of the day giving the cabin a thorough cleaning. Mama had always insisted on a clean house for the holidays. I'd never much cared one way or the other, but somehow, this year, it struck me as important. And a good cleaning was sorely needed, for with the dog come to stay and the door standing open so much of the time, well, there was loose fur and paw prints and a good deal of extra dirt and mud all over everywhere.

I was surprised when Daddy walked in, for the dog hadn't barked, and I'd been concentrating on setting the cabin to rights.

Daddy looked around at all the clean and all the new decorations, and he shook his head in a sad manner.

"Dessa Dean, you've done a fine job. Everything looks beautiful."

"Yes, sir. It's really thanks to the dog. She collected the pinecones; all I did was add ribbon."

"Well, I wish I had a Christmas dinner to contribute, but I haven't. Reckon I'll bring in some deer hocks, and maybe you can make a nice soup tomorrow."

"Oh!" Why, I'd forgotten all about the rabbit. "Close your eyes, Daddy."

"Come again?"

"Close your eyes just for a minute. The dog's

brought a Christmas present for all of us."

"Dessa Dean." And his voice was impatient and worn. "I've got more important things to tend to than a pinecone from a dog."

"Daddy, please? It is something important. Important and wonderful."

"Hmph."

But he closed his eyes just the same.

Without saying a word, I waved for the dog to come over next to me, and together we fetched the skillet that held the rabbit. I'd chipped ice and snow from the porch and packed it around the rabbit and covered the skillet with a towel to keep it a surprise.

Now, I carefully lifted the dishtowel and carried the frying pan, using both hands so it wouldn't tip, and stepped eight steps back to where Daddy stood, his shoulders slumped, one red, chapped hand covering his eyes. The dog marched alongside of me.

"All right. You can open up now."

And he did, and he looked from my face into the skillet and pushed out a puff of air from his nose and looked down at the dog.

"Well, I'll be. She caught that?"

"She did! She caught Christmas dinner for us."

"You're some dog," he said, and without hesitating, he reached out and petted her head. "Dessa Dean, see she gets an extra portion of dinner. Hunters have to keep their strength up."

That girl was so surprised she didn't growl or even set her ears back. She just let him praise her and pet her.

But even kind words from Daddy were not enough to keep her quiet out on the cold porch come bedtime.

She whined. She howled and growled and cried pitifully.

"Daddy?" I made my voice a whisper, though I knew he wasn't asleeping.

He grunted.

"Daddy, couldn't the dog sleep in here just for tonight, and we'd keep the door open a crack?"

"Bad habit to start."

"But tomorrow's Christmas. And she did bring us Christmas dinner. We'd be looking forward to bone soup if it wasn't for her."

A long quiet came from Daddy.

And eventually, a big sigh came from over his way.

"Fetch me the hammer and two or three nails. I'll

tack up a quilt and at least slow the cold air down some."

That dog was plain glad to come in. She went directly over to the stove, turned around three times, and flopped down. But once Daddy had the quilt up, and it hid the door crack, well, she began to fret and whine. Over to the door she padded and lay down before the quilt and pushed her nose under so she could smell the open air, and that's where she stayed the entire night.

Long after the dog was settled and long after Daddy had begun to snore, I lay awake waiting. Waiting till I was pretty certain it was past midnight and therefore officially Christmas Day. Every single year I had bided the time with Mama, and when I was real little, if I happened to drift off, Mama would always awaken me when she was certain the joyful day had begun.

To the Advent calendar we would quietly creep, and Mama would help me ease the Baby Jesus from the number twenty-four pocket and help me to snap him into the manger for his birthday.

And so, when I was pretty certain, out from beneath the warm quilts I wriggled, and on over to the Advent calendar I tiptoed seventeen tiptoes, and by the ember light from the stove, I snapped the Baby Jesus into place.

Mama's Mama's Mama's Best China

"HAPPY CHRISTMAS, Dessa Dean."

The backs of Daddy's chapped fingers, chilled with winter air, brushed light across my cheek. It was still dark in the cabin, but it was clear as day how gentle Daddy was feeling.

"Happy Christmas, Daddy," I said, and set up.

I heard the dog move from next the door, heard her claws scratch on the floor as she did a two-part stretch and heard her give a shake to comb her hair for the day.

Over she padded and licked my hand.

"Happy Christmas to you, too, dog," I said.

"Dessa Dean, I'm planning on putting in a long

day. I'll move my traps, try to improve my luck, so don't expect me till after dark."

"Yes, sir."

"I smell snow acoming, too. I brought in extra wood, but don't keep that door open any wider than you have to."

"Yes, sir."

Daddy seemed to be on a talking jag. I reckoned it must be the holiday that made him want to jaw.

"Dessa Dean, your mama would want us to have our regular celebration, so I want you to bring out the best china for Christmas supper tonight."

In the quiet darkness I sucked in my breath.

Mama's best china was away up high in the cupboard.

And it was heavy. Considerable heavy.

Mama had never allowed me to fetch it down. It had belonged to her mama, and before that, to her mama's mama, and what made it last all those years without chipping or breaking was the fact that only grown-up ladies ever laid hands to it.

"You're old enough. You'll do fine," Daddy said. "Just go slow."

He'd read my thoughts, sure.

"Yes, sir." I whispered the words into the air for I didn't feel certain of them.

Daddy stood up and clomped to the door. The traps clanged metal on metal when he hefted them up and slung them over his shoulder.

He opened the door wide, and the cold hurried in.

Daddy started out, then turned back to face me. His voice was smiling bright.

"I brought in a bone for the dog. It's setting on the cutting shelf."

"Oh! Thank you, Daddy! It'll make the best present for her. Won't she be tickled."

"Hmph. Do your twelve times twelve," he said.

And he set out.

As for myself, I hightailed it out from beneath the quilts, jumped into my clothes, and fixed up the dog's and my morning meal right away. I was anxious to shoo her out the door so I could set to working on her Christmas present in secret.

The blamed dog, though, had contrary thoughts. She wanted a leisurely breakfast. In fact, she insisted on *two* leisurely breakfasts, and then, why, didn't she set to digging a hole and tramping down the wood floor before the stove. She plumb ignored me every time I sashayed to the door and said inviting things such as: "Why, dog, the sun's up now, and I believe I see a mouse out there just abegging to be caught." And, "Why, the snow looks just right for bouncing around in this morning, don't you think, dog?" And, "You'd better go on out now, dog, for Daddy says there's snow on the way, and you won't want to traipse out in a storm."

That dog had a mind of her own, though. I couldn't get her to budge, so I started work on Daddy's present since he had cooperated and left the cabin when he ought.

I pulled the step stool in front of the kitchen cupboard where Mama always kept all the baking ingredients and climbed up onto its topmost step. All the way to the back of the bottom shelf I reached, behind the flour, the salt, behind all the small tied bundles of dried herbs.

I brought out a full burlap bag of sugar; the heavy glass bottle of corn syrup; seven walnuts; and, most precious of all, the two thick bars of chocolate that Mama had convinced Daddy to buy a way last summer.

I knew from the hot, dry days of summer to the cold of winter was plenty of time for him to forget we'd ever bought the chocolate down in town. 'Course, the way things had turned out, Daddy'd had a lot more on his mind than I would ever have figured. I had been 100 percent certain back then that his present would be a surprise; now I was, well, I was close to 200 percent sure.

I scootched the dog three scootches back from the stove so I could stoke it up, and pushed in a good, fat piñon log. Then, I scooped up the walnuts and carried them out to the front stoop and cracked them into little pieces with Daddy's hammer. I picked out the meat bits from the shell bits and carefully brushed the shells off the stoop and kicked snow over them. I didn't want to leave any clues that might set Daddy's mind to wondering and becoming curious if he happened home before dark.

The corn syrup and the sugar I set to boil on the stove in Mama's heaviest pot, the very heaviest pot so the sugar wouldn't scorch, just as Mama had taught me. With the long-handled wooden spoon, slowly and with all my might, I set to stirring and pushing the thick syrup into the sugar. Honest, I thought my arm would fall off it took so much mixing to get the sugar and syrup to blend.

When finally the sugar was melted, I broke the chocolate bars into small hunks and dropped them in the pot. I couldn't hold back popping one little piece into my own mouth. I didn't chew it at all, but let it melt oh so slow on my tongue.

Adding the chocolate to the pot called for more stirring; I tried with my left arm so as to give my right a rest, but it acted plain awkward and ignorant and wasn't much good at all.

At long last all the ingredients were blended, chocolate-colored the whole way through, so I plopped in the walnut pieces and stirred a bit more. Then, I poured the fudge into one of Mama's square baking pans, covered it with a clean dishtowel so dirt wouldn't blow onto it and varmints wouldn't track through it, and set it on the front stoop to harden. Right on the wolf's head plank.

I stepped fifteen steps back inside and over to the stove and stood before the dog.

The dog slept.

I folded my arms and tapped my toe on the floor.

The dog continued on.

"Dog," said I, "I finished making Daddy's present.

I need to get to work on yours now. Today is Christmas. Dog."

Her eyebrows puckered and her feet paddled. She was after another rabbit, sure.

So, I moved on to the next thing needed doing, which was setting the table. Back before the cupboard I dragged the step stool, and up to its top step I climbed. I opened the cupboard door and looked up and up to the top two shelves where Mama's best china set, unbroken and beautiful, in perfect stacks.

I turned my gaze to the dog and stared at her for a minute, hoping she'd wake up and want to go out.

She hadn't caught the rabbit yet, though; her big ol' paws were still arunning, and I knew she wasn't likely to give up on it anytime soon.

So, I clambered up onto the cutting counter on my knees, and then steadied myself on the side of the cupboard and stood full up. Oh, but it was high. I felt uncomfortable being so far away from the floor, kind of tippy-like. I wondered if Daddy ever felt that way, being as tall as he was.

Mama's fancy china pieces were pushed way to the far back of the cupboard, so they wouldn't ever accidentally fall out. I reached my hand up to the top shelf above my head; there were the dinner plates. I would need to fetch down two of them.

On top of the plates was the gravy boat. *Maybe*, I thought, *maybe I should reconsider and make a nice stew with potatoes cut up in it instead of mashed. Then I wouldn't need the gravy boat. And, instead of the dinner plates, I could use the china soup bowls, which are on the lower shelf.*

I had myself a good ways talked into that plan when my stubborn streak showed up without my even asking it to. *Dessa Dean, Mama would want you to make the best dinner you were able for Daddy, this year especially. Stew won't do.*

And I knew I was right.

I let out with a big breath that blew my bangs into the air, and clutching at the edge of the cupboard with one hand, I sent my other seeking out the gravy boat again. My fingers curled around its slim ring of a handle, and, honest, I took such a stranglehold on it, it was a wonder it didn't break right off. Out I eased the delicate piece, and down I squatted, and to the very back of the counter I scooted it. Carefully, I backed myself onto the step stool and got my feet steady on the floor again before picking up the gravy boat. With both hands I carried it to the table and with both hands, oh so slow, I lowered it to the very center of the table, where it would be safest. Then I stepped back, wiped my palms on my britches, and let my eyes fill up with the delicate beauty of the china's pattern.

Like all the set, the gravy boat was white in background; and soft, pink roses rambled lightly over it. Real, hundred percent, genuine gold trimmed its edges in a slim, perfect line. It was beautiful. And it made me think of Mama, which set my heart to aching.

I made myself get back to business, though, and marched back to the step stool.

Fetching out the dinner plates from the cupboard made my stomach twitch, for they were real large and required both my hands to bring them down. I kept feeling for the edge of the counter with one foot, for I was scared I'd step too far and tumble off backward, and that would be the end of me *and* the plates.

I was strongly relieved when I was able to lay them down at Daddy's and my places at the table, well back from the edge.

The hard part was done, to my way of thinking, and

even though the large meat platter was so heavy it made my arms shake to lift it out the cupboard, it was still a good sight easier fetching it from the middle shelf than fetching the plates from the top one. After that, I brought out two fine crystal glasses with dainty flowers etched all the way around their middles, and I set out the fine crystal candlesticks that matched them and slid the thin, brown beeswax candles into them that Mama and I had pressed and rolled. Lastly, out came the small platter that I was fixing to use for Daddy's fudge. The dinner table looked so fine and fancy, it was Christmas for sure. I felt some pride that I hadn't broken or chipped or knocked anything up. I believed Mama would be mighty satisfied with the care I'd taken, too. I knew if I stood still much longer, I'd start feeling blue, and I didn't want to. Not at all. So, I told my eyes to look over at the dog. It was high time she woke up and did something constructive.

"Dog," I said. "It's high time you woke up and did something constructive. I'm never going to get your present ready with you lollygagging before the stove the entire day. Wake up!"

And she did.

"Ow-owwww!" And out the door she trotted.

The Fudge, the Bone, and the Rabbit

THANK GOODNESS, I told myself, and set to heating up some bacon grease in the large skillet. I plopped in a cup's worth, or eight ounces is another way to say the same, and watched the grease turn from thick white to soupy gray as it melted down. When it was good and hot I set the deer leg bone into the skillet and basted it with the grease. There was still a little meat on the bone that would make it extra special for the dog, I reckoned. When it was heated through and basted seventeen times and drenched almost to drowning in bacon grease, I plopped the bone into a baking pan and slid it into the oven, adding a log to the oven portion of the stove to heat it up to baking temperature. My plan was to roast that bone good and long so all the bacon fat soaked in deep. Then, I'd let it cool and start the whole process over again, so the thick bone would be double doused. That dog was going to be so happy, I swear.

While I was waiting on the bone, I sixteen-stepped it out to the front porch to the wolf's head plank to check on Daddy's fudge. The candy was hardened up just perfect, so I carried the baking pan inside to the cutting shelf. I drew out Mama's longest slicing knife from the silverware drawer and practiced some fractions on Daddy's fudge. Down the middle I made the first cut; that made it two halves. Then, I halved the halves, so there were four parts. That is to say, quarters. Then, I halved the quarters so they were eighths, and then I spun the pan a quarter turn and set to slicing in the other direction, the horizontal direction. Only five short-ways slices would fit so the pieces would still be a good size and not all teeny-tiny and miserly, so that's how many cuts I made. It added up to forty-eight pieces of fudge, or four dozen squares, or eight times six, which reminded me I still had not come up with a twelve-times-twelve problem to finish up the twelve times table.

With the very pokey tip of the slicing knife, I lifted out each hard square of fudge and arranged it all into a pyramid, like from ancient Egypt, on Mama's small, fancy china platter. All the pink roses were covered so just the thin, smooth line of gold circled the fudge; it was a sight.

As I stood taking it in, why, all of a sudden, for just a little moment, it was like Mama was with me, right alongside of me, admiring my work on the present we'd talked over and planned for when she was still living and expecting to live some more. I felt myself smiling while at the same time a tear tickled its way down my cheek and fell onto the table.

I brushed my cheek dry and kept on; the baking bone was filling up the cabin with a warm, meaty smell. Out from the oven I brought it with a folded dishtowel so I wouldn't burn my fingers, and I set the pan on the stovetop. That bone was browning up fine. I carried it out to the wolf's head plank of the porch to cool it down quick-like so I could get it basted again and dried before the dog decided to come home.

Fixing Daddy's fudge and making the bone up for

the dog turned my mind to wondering once again if *I* would have a present. Mama had always let me have my gift soon as I was up on Christmas morning. Mayhap since Daddy had just set out as usual this morning, mayhap there wouldn't be a gift for me this year. A sad started up inside me.

But, Dessa Dean, I told myself, *don't be ungrateful; you already got the very best present you could ever have by that dog coming to stay.*

And that thought cheered most of me, but honest, a corner of my heart still wished for the surprise and jubilation Mama's presents had always provided me.

I glanced up at the sky. It was a smooth, warm blue, but dark clouds were pushing on over the mountain-top, a breeze was picking up, and I smelled snow acoming, just as Daddy had said.

The rabbit would require about an hour's cooking time, I figured, and that meant I'd best get to work dressing it and getting the vegetables chopped and ready. Thinking on the feast that was to come later made my mouth start to water and set my belly to growling, so I left the bone to cool on the porch and went back inside, where I slathered up a medium-thick slice of bread with honey and warmed my parts before the stove while I ate.

As soon as my belly hushed its growling, I let off eating, for I wanted to save as much room as I could for the rabbit and the mashed taters and . . . what else? A meal so fancy required something mighty special for dessert. I could open a can of peaches; I knew Daddy would like it. But somehow, that didn't seem quite fancy enough. With all the work I'd gone to, decorating and cleaning and fudge-making and bone-basting, and with the fact that the dog had provided us such a wonderful main course, well, opening a can just didn't seem fit.

Brown Betty were the words that popped into my head. And wouldn't that be just the perfect thing to finish the feast, but I'd have to get busy if I was to get all those apples sliced on top of the rest of the doings that still had to be done.

So, quick like a bunny I brought in the dog's bone and melted down more bacon grease and basted the bone up but good. Back into the oven I popped it, and stoked the fire with another good-sized piñon log.

There was still more mixing to do, which was the

last thing my right arm wanted to hear about. It wasn't so taxing, though, as making candy, for all I had to do was stir oats and brown sugar and cinnamon together—dry with dry ingredients combine with each other a sight easier than dry with wet. The same holds true for wet with wet being easier to mix up. Anyhow, I sorted a half-dozen small, green apples from out the storage bin; they were a mite wrinkled, but not so bad, and I sliced them up as quick as I could without endangering a finger.

Into the oats I cut plenty of cold lard and spread the bottom of another of Mama's square baking pans with half of that. The apple slices I laid out atop the oats, and I sprinkled them just ever so lightly with vinegar. Then came the rest of the oat mixture. I swear, my mouth was watering. I set the pan on the dinner table alongside Daddy's fudge, for it would only require one hour's baking time, and I needed the cutting shelf space for my next job. Namely, chopping up the vegetables.

I brought out six taters. I knew we wouldn't eat that many mashed up at one setting, but I was thinking ahead, like Mama'd taught me to do, to using the leftovers for fried potato cakes the next morning. I brought out a squash, I brought out two turnips, I brought out four carrots and a fat onion and set to peeling and chopping. The smell of all the vegetables was so sweet as I cut them up, it was like stepping back to autumn when Mama and I had dug them from the garden. I sampled them all.

A pan of water I set to boil on the stovetop for the taters, and I shoveled all the rest of those delicious garden vegetables into Mama's biggest skillet, piling them high along the sides and leaving the middle clear for the rabbit. I scurried over to the oven and brought out the dog's bone, which had baked to a dark, dark brown. I swear, there was at least a half-inch of bacon grease cooked into it. Out to the porch I shuttled it again, to cool and set.

The sky was hidden behind the dark clouds that had settled in like they owned the place. I felt a mite concerned about what was keeping the dog; she'd been out a long time, but I figured maybe she was trying to surprise us with another rabbit. I wanted to call her home, but the bone wasn't ready yet, and I sure-fire didn't want to spoil her Christmas surprise, so I just walked myself fourteen steps back inside and cut the rabbit into eight good-sized pieces and arranged them in the center of the skillet. Before I put the lid on, I added two cups of water, that would be sixteen ounces, and I crumbled up some dried thyme and sage and basil from Mama's herb bundles and sprinkled the tiny leaf bits all over everything in the frying pan. I shoved another log into the stove, just a medium-sized one so as to cook the rabbit nice and slow and not too hot. I figured on letting it get burning good before setting the rabbit to simmer, so while I waited, I pulled out one of the table chairs and sat down to rest my back for a minute.

The bone pan rattled out on the porch, and I glanced up to see a shadow cross the crack in the door.

I felt happy and sad at the same time. Happy 'cause the dog was home and sad 'cause, sure, she'd found the bone out there cooling.

"Well, come on in, dog," said I. "Guess you'll have your Christmas a little early. No harm done."

Christmas Lost

B UT SHE DIDN'T COME.

"Dog?"

There was just a big quiet in response.

I leaned forward and peered at the door.

"Dog? Is that you, girl?" A prickle began at my fore-head and ran over the top of my head and down my neck, and all the little hairs back there sprang up straight.

A snuffling noise and a low mumble started up on the other side of the door, and not in the dog's voice, either.

Well, sir, it suddenly felt as if my legs and body had melted away to nothing, and all that remained of me were my eyes and my ears.

I heard the dog's bone roll loud across the planks. And then came the noise of crunching and splintering. Something mighty big and powerful was chomping up the dog's Christmas present.

I sat with my ears taking in the champing and chawing. I sat with my eyes sprung wide, staring at the door as real slow-like, a tan, rubbery sniffer and a long cinnamon-colored snout poked around its edge.

I knew right then, every inch of me knew, there was a whole, entire bear about to come inside the cabin.

Onto my feet I jumped, so hard and fast my leg bones shot through with a pain, and the table chair I'd been setting in crashed over sideways onto the floor. I was full-out surprised to feel my legs had come back and were running and taking the rest of me with them as far from the door as they could get.

My eyes darted around the cabin, begging for a hiding place.

Under my cot? I thought for a split second on how easy a bear paw could reach under there from four different directions, and decided not.

Back toward the door I turned to see just how much of the bear had made it into the cabin so far, and the answer was: the whole entire. She was the biggest sow I'd ever seen, longer than my cot but oh so skinny. There was a starved look in her eye, and she was staring right at me.

Her long, black claws rat-a-tat-tapped on the wood floor as the bear started forward, but then she paused, her nose high in the air, sniffing and asniffing. Side to side she swung her wide head, following the variety of dinner smells from the cutting shelf, from the table, from the stovetop.

It came to me that I should take advantage of her distraction to put more distance between us, but my legs seemed to be all done running; they felt like lead and could only manage a slow backing up, no matter how I yelled at them in my head. In just five shaky steps, the backs of my legs were pressed against the Christmas trunk, and there was no more backing I could do, fast or slow.

The bear started across the floor again, rat-a-tap, rat-a-tap. Her rubber nose twitched, sniffing, stretching out toward me.

Those gold bear eyes stuck onto mine, and a growl, deep and plain mean-sounding came out from her. She was sizing me up, sure, trying to figure if she'd still have room for dessert after she finished me off.

My hands fidgeted behind my back, scrambling over the top of the trunk, trying to run away, and my mind was trying to run, too: I couldn't focus on anything practical like surviving, but just kept thinking over and over how I still needed to come up with a twelve-times-twelve problem or I'd be in hot water with Daddy.

And then, even though my brain wasn't thinking clear, my hands seemed to be, for in their skittering over the trunk, they hit on the edge of the lid, and now, they yanked it up and open, and that brought my brain around. *Get in* is what my brain came up with, so into the teeny cave of the trunk I climbed and pulled that lid down tight, tight, tight over me.

I sat stock-still in the small dark, my knees drawn up tight to my chest, my face hiding on top of them. Hard against my ribs my heart knocked; my raggedy breath gasped in and out loud, loud. Too loud.

Rat-a-tat-tap, rat-a-tat-tap started filling up my ears from outside of the trunk. She was coming for me.

The little crack of space between the lid and the box went dark as the bear's large self moved in front of it. A deep, hungry snuffle was going on right next my ear, just the other side of that thin wood. And the snuffling was pulling my scent deep into the bear. Up and down the crack her nose traveled, sniffing and sniffing me.

I squinched myself flatter against the bottom, and then, honest, I tried to prepare myself for when the bear figured how to open the trunk, and I'd be looking into the bear's gullet.

But, don't you know, the rat-a-tap moved off, and the light shone again through the crack. That bear was deserting me!

What came to my ears next, though, why, it hurt almost as much as getting eaten would, I reckoned. It was a loud, breaking, shattering crash. It was the sound of Mama's china hitting the hard floor.

I put my eye to the slit and looked out into the cabin proper. What I saw was that dad-blamed cinnamon bear finishing up the last of my perfect squares of fudge. She'd nosed the gravy boat off the table already, and it was splintered into a million zillion heartbreaking pieces. As I watched, she stretched her snout long, to reach the unbaked brown Betty. Up on her haunches she rose, her skin was so loose it drooped down around her middle. The she-bear leaned heavy on the edge of the dinner table, balancing herself while she gobbled the brown Betty, and the table started to rock back and forth, and then it tipped toward the bear. The sow gave a grunt and backed up, and over went the dinner table, and right along with it went the platters, the plates, the crystal glasses, the candlestick holders, and the candles.

Even though my arms jumped out, unbidden, to catch it all, to stop it and keep my mama's mama's mama's best china safe, it still all sailed off the edge and crashed to the floor and broke. Broke into chips and sparkling, raggedy etched posies, and jagged pink roses, and each and every one seemed to cut a deeper hole in my heart.

My eyes watered up bad as I watched that cinnamon bear waddle, without paying no never mind at all, through Mama's smashed china, licking her chops after scarfing down Daddy's present and our fancy dessert. Right on over to the stove she traipsed, rat-a-tat-tapping with her long claws. Right on over to where the taters were piled ready to put into the boiling water and right on over to where set the frying pan filled with Mama's garden vegetables and the very special Christmas present the dog had brought us.

The cinnamon bear set up on her back feet again and stuck her long snout into the steam rising above the pot. She gave a yowl and backed up. She had burned her no-good nose in the hot steam.

She lumbered over to the other side of the stove, and real dainty-like, nibbled every hunk of tater off the plate.

The skillet piqued her interest then, and she nosed its lid off. I turned away from the crack and lowered my head onto my knees once more, and the clattering lid became the wailing wind as a daymare swooped down to claim me. I felt myself pulled deeper and deeper into the biting cold and the blinding white snow.

But of a sudden, away beyond the cruel wind, another sound, a new sound, cut through the muffling veil of the blizzard.

It was the bark of a dog.

Oh, Lordy, no! I yelled inside my head, and the snow disappeared and the wind hushed, and there I was back in the Christmas trunk. I pressed my eye to the crack.

What I saw first was that dad-gum bear setting up on her haunches next the stove. She held the skillet in her big ol' front paws and was licking the last drizzles of juice from its bottom.

The rabbit was gone, bones and all.

Every last chunk of squash, turnip, and carrot had disappeared inside the bear.

My gaze slid off her and settled on the beautiful brown head of the dog, over by the door. Her mouth was opened wide as the bear's, and she was barking like it was Daddy she was facing down and not a wild beast. Her white teeth were bared, her pale brown lips pulled back to show them off.

The bear snarled at her but didn't move, just stuck her snout back into the frying pan. Not one iota of our Christmas fixings was she willing to give up.

Holding her bark, the dog stared at the bear for a long minute, and I reckoned it was because she was unused to getting no response to her threats. Then, as I watched, the dog started sniffing around the cabin floor, and at first I thought she was going over to the bear's side and was looking for food.

I should have known better.

She followed her nose right over to where I was ahiding in the trunk, and her big, brown self filled up the crack between lid and box.

"Dog," I whispered, "you get on outside and just wait for that she-bear to leave on her own. I don't want you messing with her."

The dog let out a tiny whine and sniffed her nose up and down the crack.

I heard metal clatter to the floor. The bear had finished up and dropped the frying pan.

"Dog, go on outside, *please*."

But the dog didn't. She left off sniffing me and turned back toward the bear.

A low growl started humming in her throat; and along her back, I saw her hackles rise. Slow, slow, she crept toward the bear.

The blamed bear looked like she would hold her ground. But the dog circled till she was behind the bear and then let out with a terrific bark and began to lunge back and forth, jumping in toward the sow, nipping at her heels.

The bear turned on all fours. Part way up on her hind legs she rose, and without saying a word, swiped at the dog with her huge front paw, catching her smack in the ribs.

30

Blood!

THE DOG'S YELP filled up the cabin, and she tumbled head over heels until she banged into the table leg and stopped.

But right back on her feet she sprang, snarling at the bear, lunging and circling, going for the sow's heels again. This time her teeth seemed to find a soft spot.

The bear gave out a howl, and without a second look at the dog, she humped toward the door.

The dog was at the bear's heels, nipping and yipping to speed her up. Out the door the sow bounced, banging into the doorframe in her rush to leave.

I pushed the trunk lid up, pulled my woolen cap

down hard, and clattering through all Mama's broken china, I ran to the cabin door. The light was dim due to the heavy blanket of clouds, but I could still make out the bear galumping toward the first stand of piñons and junipers with the dog hot on her trail, that one daft leg swinging out on its own trying to head the bear off from the north. The dog's angry bark echoed back to me through the biting cold air.

"No, dog!" I hollered loud.

But she paid no mind.

"Oh, no, dog," I whispered as she disappeared into the woods.

I dashed inside and snatched my coat from the chair and quicklike ran back onto the porch. I had to go after the dog, had to fetch her home afore she got hurt.

Over the wolf's head plank I darted and jumped over my birthday scratches plank, and there I was at the edge.

I stepped one foot into the air and leaned my body out, intending to go.

But my head began to spin and my heart to pound so that I staggered backward. I banged against the cabin wall and let it hold me up. I sucked in a breath and pushed it out and gulped in another.

And back I went and shot my foot off the porch again.

My ears gripped me like steel traps; I clamped my hands over them and set down on the porch edge. I scootched so my right leg was hung off the edge clear to my hip, and I forced my foot to set flat on the snowy ground.

"I've got to go," I whispered it fierce to myself. "I've got to get the dog. I'm going to get her." My voice sounded like a warning. "I'm going." I faced front and stuck my other leg over the edge and scootched until it dangled full and my left foot set solid on the ground next to the right.

"Here I go to get the dog." My voice was high and wavy sounding. And in my head, I said to myself, *If the dog can go like that with her bum leg, I can! I can!*

My ears screamed at me not to, to get on back indoors, but I didn't listen. I held them tight against my head and stood up on both feet. My whole entire self seemed to be made of lead. I tried to lift one foot to take a little step, but I couldn't get my knee to bend, and the only way my foot would go up in the air was by my leaning my body way far back.

I took one soldier step and then a second, and the trees and the clouds went into a whirl so I couldn't keep my body upright. Down to my knees I crumpled. The tingly, whisking away feeling of a daymare swept over me, and I heard a high voice cry out "No! I'm not daft, I'm not." And then I felt my hands and my knees scraping over icy snow as I crawled back to the porch.

I leaned heavily against the wall of the cabin and forced my shaking legs back under me so I was stand- ing. I trudged inside to the stove, where the pot of water was still boiling merrily. I dropped into a limp heap, and I cried and cried for being the scaredy baby I was, for not rescuing the dog when she had risked herself to rescue me, but there was no sound to my cry- ing, only hot, shamed tears that wouldn't stop.

After a time, my eyes dried up, and I rolled over bits of precious china onto my side away from the fire. A raggedy sigh billowed up from deep inside me. I stared at an egg-sized spot on the wood floor.

It was a long minute before I really saw the spot, and it was another long one more before my mind took in what it truly was I was staring at.

Blood. It was blood.

I scrambled to my feet and peered down at it. Was it the bear's blood? Or was it—"Oh, no-no." My voice was a moan. "Not the dog, oh, Lordy, please, not the dog."

My insides bunched up picturing the dog trailing blood through the woods, losing her strength drop by drop on the snow. Lying down to rest, and then trying to get up again and not able to. Clear as day I pictured giant, white flakes drifting down from the dark sky, settling over her, freezing her just like— "No!" It was a scream, and it made me jump.

Without counting a step, I skittered over to the nails in the wall and lifted my knapsack down. An old spiderweb that had been cast between it and the wall pulled loose with a wispy tearing sound, but I didn't bother brushing it away. I cut a goodly chunk off the bread loaf, wrapped it in one of Mama's clean dish-towels, and from Daddy's special bin where he kept the food he packed to see him through his traipsing high in the mountains each day, I grabbed four pieces of deer jerky. If—*when* I found the dog, I reckoned she might be in need of nourishment. I took a fistful of clean rags to use as bandages in case the dog was injured, but, *Oh, Lordy, please don't let her need them,* is what I thought as I poked the rags and all the rest into my knapsack.

And then, well, I marched back to the blood spot and stared at it, took the look of it deep inside myself. Down beside it I knelt and stuck the pad of my pointer finger into it and felt its sticky coldness, out of the body where it didn't belong. I looked at my finger and memorized the orange thinness of it.

I stood, buttoned my coat, slid the straps of the knapsack over my shoulders, put Mama's beautiful knit gloves on my hands, yanked down my itchy woolen cap, pulled up my stubborn streak harder than I could ever remember pulling it before. I turned for one last look at the cabin, and my eyes lit on the angel set on the bookshelf, gazing at the mess that was left. And though I knew it couldn't be, her beautiful face seemed to have taken on a pained look. I couldn't bear it. Real gentle-like, I picked the angel up, wrapped her in the rags in my knapsack and buckled her in safe.

"I'm not daft!" I said it loud into the empty cabin.

And out the door I stepped.

31

A 12 x 12 at Long Last

I T WAS THE FAR SIDE of mid-afternoon, but even though the sun was hardly making any effort, I still squinched my eyes till they were almost closed, trying to hide the fact from them that I was outside. I kept my slitted eyes pointed at the ground, and I kept hold of the cabin wall all the way around to the back where my snowshoes hung on two tenpenny nails next to Daddy's.

Over and over right out loud in the air I said, "The dog needs me. That girl needs me," so as to make sure not just my brain heard it, but my ears as well.

I kept my head lowered as I lifted the snowshoes down and strapped them on my feet, and once again I kept touch with the cabin wall till I'd made it back around to the porch. But that was as far as the cabin could take me.

I pulled in a sharp breath and raised my gaze just far enough to find the first set of the dog's tracks, and just beyond them, the bear's. There! Two spots of blood stained the snow. But the drops were between the bears' back paw prints and the dog's front. I still couldn't tell who was hurt.

"The dog needs me," I said, and the wind whisked my words away so quick I was afraid I'd forget them, so over and over with only a breath between, I repeated them. "The dog needs me. That girl needs me."

I trudged on after the bear and the dog; not every set of prints showed blood, but when there was a drop or two, it was always betwixt the animals, sometimes closer to the bear, sometimes closer to the dog, never giving me a clue.

I didn't allow my eyes to stray beyond the very next set of tracks, for I knew if I did, I would see how big the outdoors was and how small I was in comparison.

But the tracks just made a beeline for the woods, and it wasn't long, following such a straight course, that my mind began to wander. I could feel a panic lurking, and I knew if I looked too close at it, I'd make a dead run back for the cabin, leaving the dog to the bear. I couldn't let that happen, so I gave my brain a hard jerk, and, in searching for something to occupy it, I hit upon my undone twelve-times-twelve problem. And suddenly, ideas started popping up like Mama's tulips in the spring. For example: If a big, fat, no-account cinnamon bear came into our cabin on Christmas Day and chomped our rabbit down in twelve bites, and if she got twelve bad stomach cramps for every single bite of stolen meat she took, why, how many belly cramps did that old sow have to suffer? The answer is one hundred and forty-four cramps, and this problem just goes to show that 12 x 12 is 144.

"The dog needs me. That girl needs me."

And: If a good-for-nothing cinnamon bear barged uninvited into our cabin on Christmas Day and broke up all the precious china that had belonged to my mama's mama's mama, and the bear got a full twelve china splinters in her paw with each step she took, well, how many steps did she have to take before she had 144 of my mama's shattered china pieces in her dad-blamed foot paining her something awful? The answer is twelve steps, which just goes to show that 12 x 12 = 144.

"The dog needs me. That girl needs me."

Honest, I felt some satisfaction that I'd finally finished up my schoolwork, and I let my eyes raise to take my bearings.

I was deep in the woods, and while I could still make out the dog's tracks and the bear's ahead of hers, the light was mostly gone. I couldn't make out blood spots any longer; it was too dark for it.

Not only had the daylight gone, but the storm had settled in and snow was falling, thick and heavy. I turned back toward the cabin. I could make out three or four sets of the tracks back through the trees the way we'd come, but as I stared at them, the breeze stirred up to become a gusting, howling wind, and the dog's tracks, the bear's tracks, and my tracks began to smooth out and disappear below blowing, drifting snow.

My stomach pinched up, for I was too much reminded of the day Mama's tracks and mine had disappeared.

"The dog needs me. That girl needs me."

I spun back to the newest prints, but naturally, the

wind was ablowing in front of me, too. And the fresh-est tracks of the bear and the dog were quick getting covered by snow.

Fear had set to creeping dark and numbing through all my parts, and my mind was running in circles trying to come to a saving plan. Turning back, I would end up wandering lost with nothing at all to follow before long. *You are one dumb bunny, Dessa Dean, keeping your head down and not taking in landmarks or guideposts.*

Oh, hush up, I told myself, and tried to concentrate my thoughts again. Going forward, the older tracks would get covered, but there would keep being new ones to guide me, if I could just go faster, get closer to them so they would still show when I reached them. That was all I could do, I figured. And so, I began to run through the deep snow.

The wind had taken on a mournful voice, and the fat flakes of snow that had started out soft and gentle turned sharp and icy. They pelted my cheeks like shards of glass, like bits of broken china. My eyes watered up so I could barely see, but I kept on and on.

And as ever more shallow and streaky the bear's prints became, the dog's became.

At long last I stopped and stared down with all my might and concentration to pick up on the next set of tracks.

But there wasn't another.

There was nothing but snow. Only snow. Smooth snow, snow that hadn't been tracked through or walked on or even skimmed over. Just snow.

I looked far ahead into the night, but there was only snow. Snow so thick I couldn't breathe without taking it into my nose and throat, snow so thick that the pine trees appeared just for the blink of an eye before the swirling and blowing made them invisible again.

I spun back the way I had come. The way I thought I had come.

Snow.

And then the whole entire world began to spin, and I couldn't bear the circling of the snow and the twirling feeling behind my eyes.

Down to my knees I sank, and the cold seeped through my britches and deep into my legs, holding them fast to the ground.

The wind shoved me this way and that, like a bully, and its voice seemed to taunt me and sting my aching ears with words, howling words, words I'd heard before.

"Scaredy baby! Jack Frost is coming. Just you wait, scaredy girl; he's coming, sure." And icy and solid as Mama's hand, the wind smacked me across the face, knocking me over sideways into the deep, drifted snow.

32

Jack Frost

"MAMA!" I WAILED IT out right next to her ear. "Josephine Elvira Hubbard, get up! Mama, get up, get up. We have to keep moving or we'll freeze. Please, Mama, please, Mama, please, Mama, please, Mama."

I knew in all the chilled corners of my heart that calling, hollering, pleading would do no good. I knew Mama was froze. Jack Frost had come, and I hadn't even seen him. I looked down into Mama's dear face and saw how he'd sealed her eyes closed for good and all with lacy snow and diamond drops of ice. Jack Frost had come, and I hadn't even seen him. I reached out to Mama's cheek and felt how he'd stolen the softness of life and left the deep, padded coldness of death in its place.

"Please, Mama, please, Mama, please, Mama."

The words kept coming, in a chant, over and over as I oh so gently brushed the snow from Mama's forehead, off her eyelids, off her chin, from her forehead, off her eyelids, off her chin, fighting off Jack Frost the only way I still could, by keeping Mama atop the snow, refusing him the frozen tomb he intended.

A gust of Jack Frost's wind blew frozen snow into my eyes, trying to blind me so he could get on with burying Mama, but I wouldn't let him. I wouldn't. I squeezed my eyes tight shut against his icy needles.

"Please, Mama, please, Mama, please, Mama, please, Mama."

My blind hand reached out for Mama's forehead, and I brushed and I brushed for ever so long, until all of me was numb and heavy, and no matter how I tried, my arm would not lift one more time. With the last bit of strength I could muster, I lay down over Mama, shielding her as best I could.

"Please, Mama, please, Mama, please, Mama."

My voice was not even so big as a whisper against

the howling wind. I pressed my cheek to Mama's and the snow that had settled on her frozen face turned to water and ran down my cheek like tears.

A long time later, the changing sound of the wind woke me. It whined soft and sad next my ear. I stretched my hand out to Mama's cheek to start in brushing the snow away once more, but it wasn't Mama's cheek my hand touched. I quick snatched it back, for what it had brushed up against was cold, but not dead. It sure-fire wasn't Mama. Panic reared up in my chest, capturing my breath, for the thought came to me that it must be Jack Frost himself. Oh so scared, but not able to stop myself, I unscrewed my eyes the teensiest bit and let them peek out.

Jack Frost was wearing a sleek, dark-colored fur coat against the cold. Seeing that, a powerful fury welled up in me, for he couldn't even bear the frozen air he himself had brought. *Coward!* I thought. I let my anger ball up like a fist and it shot down my arm so I gave him a mighty shove.

"Coward!" I screamed at him.

"Boof."

My eyes flew wide and I stared. It took my daymare-and-cold-addled brain a long second to recognize it wasn't Jack Frost come. It was the dog.

The dog had come!

I tried to sit up quick, but a heavy quilt of snow lay over me like a shroud, and I had to force my way up through *it* and the haze and weakness of my daymare. I was panting by the time I got set up. In slow motion I reached for the dog and drew my arms about her neck. Her warm tongue on my cheeks, on my nose, on my eyelids thawed me out and brought me full into the present.

"Oh, dog," I said. My lips were heavy and my tongue thick with cold. "You're all right. You're all right." I gave her another weak hug about the neck.

"Ra."

I looked up, past the dog's broad head into the dark. The deep dark of the night. The snow still fell heavy, the wind still churned and drifted it into humps and walls and shallow trenches.

"Dog, we're lost," I whispered, and the words made my heart let go its joy at seeing her and drop down low and hopeless again. "You lit out after the bear, and I lit out after you, and it was probably only the bear that had any idea where she was heading."

The dog set back on her haunches, and I heard her tail wag the snow back and forth.

Into the high dark she pointed her warm muzzle.

"Rroo!"

It was what she always said when she felt strongly about something.

"You're right, I'm hungry, too." I put away my low thoughts and slid the knapsack off my shoulders. My stiff fingers set to fishing deep inside it for the jerky and bread, brushing past the wooden angel in their search.

I didn't tell the dog, and I barely let the thought into my own head, but the tips of my fingers were numb; they'd got frostbite, sure. A shiver, not only of cold, but of fear zipped through me, thinking how close Jack Frost had come to claiming me.

I had to strain to grip the dried meat. I slipped a piece into the dog's mouth and then held the bread with both my hands while I tore a piece off with my teeth.

The dog asked for another strip of meat before I'd even swallowed for the first time. And she wolfed that one down, too. She didn't ask for a third, but set to nudging at my knee with her nose. I ignored her as long as I could, but her pushing got harder and harder until she was practically butting her head under my leg. She gave me such a push that I lost my balance and either had to fall over or scramble to my feet.

So, I scrambled.

The dog trotted a few feet distant from me and pointed her frosty muzzle into the night air.

"Roo!" she said.

She was thinking of getting on again. I reckoned she was still bent on tracking the bear.

"I don't think that's a good idea, dog," I said.

"Boof!"

And she trotted even further away so I could barely make out her form through the dark and the snow.

"No, don't go! Please." The words wailed out of me. I couldn't have her leave me alone again. Jack Frost would get me, sure. Or the bear would have me, if we followed it. But at least she'd be with me.

"I'll come. Hold on there. I'm coming, dog."

I struggled to get my arms through the shoulder straps of the knapsack, struggled to sling it onto my back; it seemed to weigh considerable more than it had when first I'd started out to hunt the dog.

The new snow was wet, which made it so very heavy; every step I took called for considerable effort, and my feet plain didn't want to move. I was slow, so slow.

The dog kept pulling ahead of me, and at first when I couldn't keep up, she'd give me an encouraging bark and then stand still till I'd almost caught up before she trotted off again. After a time, though, it seemed she got frustrated with my inchworm progress.

Back she came to my side and lay herself firm against my leg, so her weight pushed me into taking one step and then another.

On and on and on she kept me trudging, through waist-high drifts, between close-growing brambles that stuck just their tips out of the snow so as to scratch at my frozen cheeks. With every step, up or down or sideways, her side stayed pressed tight to my leg and moved me forward.

I couldn't any longer feel my toes, and while that made walking a sight less painful, I knew it meant Jack Frost was still tracking us, still trying to take me one part at a time.

On and on and on we kept, and a weariness heavier than the snow, more nagging than the wind crept steadily through me until I couldn't ignore it.

"Dog, I don't believe I can go any further."

I stumbled and almost fell, but the dog lifted her head against my hip and pressed herself tighter to my leg, and I took one step and then another. I stumbled over my snowshoes and over rocks, but the dog always caught me, and finally, I quit arguing with her and determined I'd go until she couldn't get me to anymore.

Suddenly, after all those steps, the tip of my snowshoe caught on something big and solid, and not even the dog could hold me up. I sprawled forward, falling headlong toward the ground, but instead of hitting snow, my chin banged down onto something that didn't give at all. Something that jarred all the teeth in my head.

I looked up into the dark and thought I was stunned from the knock, for before my eyes, a long rectangle of light suddenly flashed on, and the silhouette of a man stepped into it.

Jack Frost.

"Run, dog," I managed to squeak out, before I got scooped up and carried off.

33

Closing the Door

"DESSA DEAN?"

My ears took in Daddy's shaky voice, and then a warm, wet tongue mopped my cheek, and I knew the dog was with me as well. I stretched out both my hands, and when one had found the dog's head and the other was nestled in Daddy's own big hand, I opened my eyes and looked around.

Why, I was on my cot—before the woodburning stove—in the cabin.

I was home.

"How'd you ever find us, Daddy?" My voice was a scratchy whisper.

The look in Daddy's eyes was one of puzzlement.

"Dessa Dean, I didn't find you. The dog brought you home."

"I thought she was taking me along to find the bear."

"The bear? Is that what happened here, Dessa Dean?"

"Yes, sir, and she broke all Mama's fine china and ate our Christmas feast and your Christmas present, too, Daddy. And the dog's fine bone."

My face crinkled up, but no tears came; they'd been sucked dry by the wind and the cold.

Daddy held me tight and warm and close, and I told him through long, raggedy sobs everything that had passed. And then he told me about coming home to find the cabin in a shambles and how that had filled him with dread of what had become of me and the dog, and how he'd hurried to pack up a lantern and blankets and water in his own knapsack and had just opened the door to start a search, when, BAM! The dog had led me right to the front porch, so close I couldn't have missed it in a pig's eye.

I reached up and felt the goose egg on my forehead.

"I'm surprised that bear was so hard to chase off. She must have been half starved."

"She was mighty set on eating everything. Her skin was loose and flappy all over. It jiggled when she walked."

"She was probably holed up with the bad weather for a time and needed filling before the new storm forced her to lay low again. That's one brave dog, facing down a hungry bear like she did, Dessa Dean."

"Yes, sir. I'm grateful to her." I reached out and pulled the dog's head to mine in a little squeeze.

Daddy set a soup bone to soaking and boiling and then took a close look at all my frozen spots, and laid a stove-warmed towel to the dog's paws to help them thaw.

"Don't reckon either one of you will lose any fingers or toes, Dessa Dean. That dog got you home just in time."

"Daddy, do you find any cuts or bites on her? Somebody, her or the bear, left drips of blood all the way through the woods."

I watched Daddy gently go over every square inch of the dog, and she let him with no back talk at all.

"Must be the bear, dog's whole," Daddy said.

A big sigh of relief worked its way from deep inside of me.

After we'd all had a portion of steaming soup, Daddy turned to me, his lips pursed.

"It's a bad idea leaving that door open, Dessa Dean. Somehow, that dog's going to have to settle to the idea; I won't risk your safety again," Daddy said.

"Oh, but, Daddy," I said, "I can't make her go back to sleeping in the cold. Why, I wouldn't even be here if it weren't for the dog."

Daddy shook his head in a stubborn manner and stepped over to the door.

The dog had been curled on the floor next to me, but when she saw Daddy move, she sprang up and beat it over to him. Right in front of him she set down and barked.

"Hush, now," he told her.

"Boof!"

"Inside with the door closed, or outside with the door closed, dog. That's your choice."

"Boof."

I watched, my heart drooping low and sad filling me up.

"Stop it now," Daddy commanded.

But she didn't.

"Boof!" she yelled and stood up, the whole while staring him straight in the eye.

Her hackles rose, and she took a step closer to Daddy.

Honest, I thought she was going to take a bite out of him, and Daddy looked mighty wary himself, but he stood his ground.

"Boof, boof!" she shouted out, and then, lowering her head, she gave his leg a hard nudge, just as she had mine when she was rescuing me.

Her weight was such that Daddy had to take a little step closer to the door.

"Boof!"

He reached for it to steady himself, and when his fingers grasped the side of it, he swung it inward.

The door's creaking sounded like a grim warning to my ears.

Slam!

The door closed tight and final; the latch dropped into place.

I held my breath, waiting for Leanin' Dog to be clutched by her fear, waiting for her to go berserk.

"Boof," she said again.

And then, why, she turned around, padded over to my cot, flopped down, closed her eyes, and let out a grand sigh.

Daddy's and my eyes met and both of us had our

eyebrows raised tall, but we didn't say a word about it.

"Happy Christmas, Daddy."

"Happy Christmas, Dessa Dean."

I started to snuggle down under the quilts, but then I remembered. Watching for pieces of glass, I tiptoed over to the tenpenny nails where Daddy had hung my knapsack and lifted it down. After I'd undone the buckle, I sent my fingers inside searching. Gently, gently, I lifted the bundle of rags out and hurried back to my cot. Beneath the warm covers, I unwrapped the angel and laid her smooth self down next to my cheek. Then I lolled my arm off the edge of the cot so my hand rested flat on the dog's broad head.

"Happy Christmas, dog."

The last sound I heard before drifting off was the broom moving back and forth over the floor, sweeping up all Mama's precious china.

Hours later I woke and sat bolt upright in the dark of the cabin. My stomach was all butterflies, but it wasn't from being afraid, it was excitement. Then I reached out for the dog, and felt her setting up next my cot, leaning tight against it. I picked up her floppy ear and whispered to her, "I know your right name now. Sure-fire, I do."

34

The Dog's True Name

I T WAS STILL dark when I woke early in the morning. The dog was whining in my ear, and Daddy was stirring over by the cutting shelf. I reached out and scratched the dog's head and then threw back my quilts and crossed to the door, the dog at my heels. I creaked the door open wide enough for her to pass. The storm had moved on, the sky was sparkly with stars, and the full moon was still floating high.

Out the door the dog scooted and off the porch toward the back of the cabin.

I waited for a bit so she'd have time for her business, and then, "Leanin' Dog," I called. I felt some surprise at how sure my voice sounded.

I waited, expecting that any second my ears would fill up with her returning sounds.

Nothing.

"Leanin' Dog." I called louder and stronger.

But my ears stayed empty. A little bit of doubt crept into my mind along with all the names I'd been sure of before.

I tiptoed out to the edge of the porch and pointed myself toward the corner of the cabin and cupped my hands around my mouth.

"Leanin' Dog, come home now!"

And before I even got the last word out, my ears took in the sound of crunching snow, and my eyes soaked up the sight of the brown dog loping back around the corner to me.

The air nearly froze my teeth due to the smile that broke across my face.

"Good girl, Leanin' Dog." I hugged her hard around the neck.

"Ra," she said, and followed me inside.

I shut the door and hustled over before the stove. Daddy had it stoked up to start the day and the lantern was aglowing.

"Guess you found her true name." Daddy turned from the cutting shelf and smiled at me.

"Yes, sir," I said, and I smiled right back at him.

"That means *she's* come upon her true *home*, Dessa Dean. A dog knows when she's found a soul that understands her."

It was then my eyes lit on the dinner table. Daddy followed my gaze.

"The bear spared one glass, one candlestick holder, and that small platter of your mama's," he said.

They were all set out there, looking sparse and lonely. The small platter had a quarter-sized chip missing, its rough white inside surface showed like a wound.

"That platter was to hold your fudge, Daddy. Mama and I had it planned since last summer." My eyes began to water up.

Daddy stopped what he was doing and came over and knelt down beside me, put his arm about my shoulders.

"Dessa Dean, the very best Christmas gift I could ever have was getting you—and the Leanin' Dog— home safe. Finding the cabin in the state I did last night, well, I didn't have hardly a hope."

I looked up into Daddy's face and saw that his own eyes had tears in them.

"Oh, Daddy, I'm glad for that, too, honest. It's only that now it'll be another year to wait for Christmas, and so many of Mama's precious things broken and gone for good and all." My shoulders started to shake, and I felt my face crinkling even though I tried to hold it steady.

"Dessa Dean, come right on over here and see what." Daddy laid his hands on my shoulders and marched me gently over to the cutting shelf. His tattered canvas knapsack was laid out and the flap open. The handle of the black cast-iron skillet poked out. He opened the knapsack wide so I could see there was also a crockery water jug corked and ready to go, a big handful of garden carrots, the cup of lard, Daddy's small hatchet, and wooden matchsticks all setting inside the skillet.

Honest, I didn't understand his point.

"Are you going up the mountain for a long time, Daddy? More than just the day?"

A big sad started to make its way through me; it was bad enough missing Christmas, I didn't want to be missing Daddy, too. Not one bit.

"Nah, girl. We're going to have our Christmas dinner. No dad-gum bear is going to keep us from our feast. I'm leaving off trapping for the day, and I planned we'd go down to Willow Creek. Yesterday morning I saw the flow was stronger, and I'm betting our best fishing hole is staring to melt out some. If we're lucky, we'll catch fresh trout to fry." Daddy paused. He looked straight at me, and his eyebrows lifted; there was a hope waiting quiet in his eyes.

It had been a long time, a *long* time since I had seen hope in Daddy's eyes.

"Can we do that, Dessa Dean?"

I sucked my cheeks in tight between my teeth and felt all the scared of the last night sweep through me. I thought of Jack Frost stalking me. I thought of the daymare and having to see Mama die again. I thought about how even though I'd known what I might face by going out in the world once more, I'd still done it. And, I thought of the Leanin' Dog finding me and how tight she'd pressed against my leg, leading me home.

I looked down.

Leanin' Dog set next to me, pressed tight against my leg.

"Yes, sir, I believe we can," I said.

35

Rroo!

DADDY CLAPPED HIS hands and rubbed them together.

"All right then. Dessa Dean, climb on up and bring down two more of your mama's best china dinner plates."

I couldn't keep back the smile that wanted to come, so I didn't even try. I just pulled the step stool over and climbed to its top step and hoisted myself onto the cutting shelf and stood up next the cupboard. And when Daddy opened the door for me, I reached up high and plucked out one plate after the other and handed them down to him. Slick as anything.

Daddy brought out a wool blanket and with great

good care wrapped the plates over and over, so they'd be safe as could be and then tied the bundle up with twine and slid it gently into the knapsack.

I took out two forks and two knives of Mama's fine silverware, wrapped them in two of Mama's fanciest dishtowels, one with its edges embroidered with fine green thread, the other with red, and laid them atop the plates. Lastly, I slid the Leanin' Dog's food bowl in on top of everything.

"Dessa Dean," Daddy said, "check if there's any worms in the cornmeal to use for fish bait; otherwise, I'll have to hunt grubs under the woodpile."

I did as I was told and sifted through till I had a half dozen nice, plump ones. Daddy brought out a tiny tin box and I rolled them into it.

Daddy checked his knife was on his belt.

"Set?" he asked me.

"Yes, sir," said I.

We put on our heavy coats, and I fetched my gloves from where Daddy had set them to dry before the stove and slid my fingers into their warm coziness.

Daddy opened the cabin door, and the dog bounded outside.

I pulled down my itchy, woolen cap and stepped onto the porch.

The sun was creeping up over the canyon and turning its east-facing wall all pink, and the winter sky was going from gray to a shy blue.

I drew in a deep breath of the brand-new day's frosty air, and felt it chill my insides in a pleasing way.

My snowshoes still sprawled on the porch where Daddy'd left them lay the night before, so I set to fastening them onto my feet while Daddy retrieved his own from off the back cabin wall and fetched his cane pole from out the shed.

The dog bounded into the snow, wagging her tail and smiling at me.

"Ra!" She said.

Off the porch I stepped, and let go the cabin wall. I stood still for just a minute, waiting to see if I'd commence to feel dizzy, or if my ears would start to nag.

But, honest, nothing of the sort happened. Rather, an old happy I'd almost forgotten took to threading its way through my whole self. I turned to the climbing sun, and its warmth spread over my face like a smile.

I let the sun's smile become my own and turned it

on the dog and then on Daddy. When my eyes met his, why, what I saw ashining there was strong and pure pride, and the biggest smile I'd ever seen was settled across his face. The three of us set off toward Willow Creek in the warming air.

Even with the snow all fresh and new fallen, there were plenty of tracks in it. Three teeny voles had popped out from their tunnels beneath the snow and scurried in lines and circles, dancing a mousey dance. The dog followed her nose round and round their ballet prints, so Daddy and I both had to laugh at her turns and spins.

"Looka there, Dessa Dean. Know who belongs to those?" Daddy pointed at some tracks just ahead of us at the edge of the woods.

I felt a mite timid; it had been such a long time since I'd been out in the world to read the morning newspaper; I didn't want to let Daddy down. But over to the tracks I tramped and squatted down next to them, taking my time, taking in the details.

They were dainty in nature and kept a straight line through the snow. The front prints showed four toes, although I knew there were five on the actual animal, and they were overlaid by the back prints. That was what told me: 1) who the animal was, and 2) how fast it was agoing. The whole entire course of the track was only about three inches wide due to the leisurely pace it had chosen so the back prints set down right over the front. Every few feet the animal would stop, and there'd be a nose snuffle hole set before the paw prints.

I stood up and looked at Daddy.

"Red fox looking for breakfast not very long ago."

Daddy gave a little nod, his eyes shining, and stepped into the woods.

I looked down at Leanin' Dog. She was staring up into the brightening sky; I followed her gaze. A huge gaggle of Canada geese was flying in a picture-perfect arrowhead, right across the pale, full moon still dangling up there. As they winged closer to us, their encouraging honks filled up my ears, filled up my heart.

I smiled at the dog and she wagged back at me, and we followed Daddy into the pines and junipers.

Down through the deep, fresh snow we tramped on our snowshoes, and beside me Leanin' Dog bounded like a deer. She'd bounce till she was winded and her breath was steaming into the air, and then stop and push her brown nose deep into the snow and come up with a sparkling, white muzzle.

"Boof," she called, and ran circles.

Whenever I spotted pinecones on the boughs of the piñons, I'd stop and collect their little tan nuts, thinking of the good toasty flavor they'd add to any trout Daddy was able to catch.

We reached the creek—shimmering beneath layers and layers of ice in spots, starting to bubble out in the open in other parts. The three of us meandered with the stream down to our favorite fishing hole at a deep cut in the bank. The water was flowing fast around our spot and had caused a good-sized hole to melt out at its edge. A good-sized hole that led right down deep to where the fish were spending the winter.

Daddy laid his pole and knapsack aside, and we both set to gathering brown pine needles and small dried twigs from dead piñon branches to use for kindling.

While the dog rolled in the snow and Daddy used his hatchet to break up an old cedar stump into nice, thick logs, I set rocks for a fire ring.

It wasn't long before Daddy had the fire burning real hot, and then it was time to catch some fish. Down into water clear of ice Daddy dropped his line with a lead sinker and a worm on the small hook, and down and down it went. Before long, he'd snagged a cutthroat trout long as my lower arm. It was beautiful, all golden-brown with black speckles and orange slash marks under the gill slits. In again he cast his weighted line, and didn't he catch another winter-hungry trout that quick.

We smiled at each other and shook our heads at his great good luck, and Daddy set to cleaning them. The Leanin' Dog had been just asetting, studying on what Daddy was up to that whole time.

Now, she stood up and gave a two-part stretch real casual-like, and then gingerly, oh so slow, looking like it hurt, that dog stepped into the flow of the creek. Stock-still she stood, the water streaming around her legs, and down into our fishing hole she peered. Minutes passed and Leanin' Dog didn't move so much as a hair.

And, then, when I'd almost got bored staring at her, why, she struck like lightning—that quick. It was a beautiful sight. She jumped her front legs wide and thrust her whole entire head under water in the same split second.

Just as quick, she was back up in the air where she belonged, smiling around the big ol' cutthroat she held between her teeth.

Out from the creek she waded and shook her ears like she was trying to get rid of them and then oh so gently dropped the fish in the frying pan.

Well, sir, Daddy and I both laughed out loud, and Daddy told her he reckoned she'd won their fishing contest fair and square. I noticed, as the trout crackled and popped over the fire, that Daddy was whistling. I hadn't heard that for a long time.

As I sliced the carrots into the skillet and cracked the piñon nuts I'd gathered, sprinkling them over the browning trout, I felt plain gladsome, and I hummed a little tune myself. That was something else I hadn't heard for a long time.

Even if it was a day late, it was the finest Christmas feast ever, eating fresh-caught trout and crisp carrots off Mama's fine china out deep in the woods. After it was done, and our bellies were full, we settled back against the tree trunks and rocks, and Leanin' Dog snuggled in against my side, and we did nothing but smack our lips and take in the scenery for quite a time. Soft-looking, white clouds moved by slowly overhead; there was one that looked like a fish, another like a dog with floppy ears.

Daddy lay the last of the cedar stump on the fire, and I scootched a mite closer to warm my hands and watched the smoke drift up toward the white moon. It was then, in the quiet, that my discontent started to nag again, like a splinter of china lodged in my boot. Finally, I couldn't hold the question in a minute longer.

"Daddy?" I asked. "Would there have been something for me for Christmas if the bear hadn't got into the cabin and eaten everything?"

Well, sir, he set up so quick it spooked the Leanin' Dog. She jumped to her feet and growled into the woods. Daddy look startled himself, like he'd set on something uncomfortable.

He let out with a laugh then and shook his head. Over next to him he pulled the knapsack and reached into its outside pocket.

"Close your eyes, Dessa Dean," he told me. "And hold still."

I did as he said, and a moment later I felt my itchy woolen cap eased off my head and a crackle of static made some of my hairs stand up. I fought to keep my hands from jumping up to protect my ears from the cold. And then, why, something soft settled down over the top of my head, over my ears. Something warm and comforting.

"All right then, Dessa Dean."

I reached up and patted and smoothed both my hands all over my head. Real nice and easy and slow, I pulled the cozy covering off and brought it down before my eyes.

Oh!

What my hands held was a perfect, beautiful winter hat sewn of rabbit pelts, all soft and gray.

"Oh, Daddy." And that was all I could get out.

"Your mama made that for you," he said. "I trapped the rabbits last spring and tanned the skins, and she sewed it last summer. It's for your Christmas, Dessa Dean. It's from me and your mama."

Tears spilled out from my eyes as I snuggled the hat back onto my head and over my ears. They weren't just sad tears, though; they were tears of wonderment that even though Mama was gone, she had still managed to have a Christmas present for me. A Christmas present that felt almost like a hug. It was the most perfect gift me or anyone else in the whole wide world had ever gotten. Ever. I was sure of it.

And, it didn't itch at all.

I leaned back comfortable again and looked up at the soft, white moon. It was getting ready for bed, hanging just above the tops of the pines now. The biggest, roundest, most beautiful day-after-Christmas moon I'd ever seen.

Somewhere deep in the woods, I figured, that dad-blamed cinnamon bear was curled up beneath the same moon, sleeping off the feast we'd provided her. I sat there, and a feeling of pure disgust with the bear filled me, thinking of Mama's broken china scattered about and the feast gone. I couldn't help but let out a sigh.

"What's rankling you, Dessa Dean?" Daddy asked.

And I told him.

"Way I got it figured, that bear did us a favor. Christmas dinner's a small price to pay for what she gave us."

My mouth gaped open.

"How'd you come to that?" I asked.

"Well now, if it wasn't for that ornery bear, I doubt we'd be out here alongside Willow Creek with you taking in the world again."

I shook my head and thought of it.

"I reckon that's true," I said after a spell.

And as I pondered it further, I recognized that after all, most of Mama's dear china still set safe in the cupboard, and that while we'd sacrificed the rabbit Leanin' Dog had brought, why, we'd had just as fine a banquet of fresh trout, all of us.

The Leanin' Dog stirred by the fire, and I watched as she stood up and stretched and padded over to set down next to me.

Heavy with sleep, she leaned into me, and I leaned right back.

"Happy Christmas, Leanin' Dog," I hummed to her softly.

She swiped my nose with her tongue and raised her soft, brown muzzle into the chill morning air, pointing it up and up to the paling moon.

"Rroo!" she sang out. "Rroo!"

And I reckon I couldn't have said it any better.